RED HUNTERS AND THE ANIMAL PEOPLE

OHIYESA

FOREWORD BY
CMARIE FUHRMAN

EDITED BY
TAMMY LEWIS

WFP
WORDFIRE PRESS

Ebook ISBN: 978-1-68057-675-7
Trade Paperback ISBN: 978-1-68057-676-4
Jacketed Hardcover ISBN: 978-1-68057-677-1
Illustrations and figures are in the public domain.
Cover design by Tammy Lewis and Allyson Longueira
Cover art by egoncharov180@gmail.com | Depositphotos

Published by WordFire Press, LLC
P.O. Box 1840 Monument, CO 80132
Kevin J. Anderson & Rebecca Moesta, Publishers
WordFire Press Edition 2024 | Printed in the USA

Join our WordFire Press Readers Group for new projects and
giveaways. Sign up at wordfirepress.com.

RED HUNTERS AND
THE ANIMAL PEOPLE

CONTENTS

FOREWORD

I was asked once, "Do stories lie waiting in place for a writer, or does a place awaken the story in the writer?" "Both," I replied. I think this would have been Ohiyesa's reply as well, for in the pages that follow, a union occurs, a union that has been present and remains present in Native stories and Native storytelling, a union between land, animal people, and humans.

I sometimes wonder where we, as a nation, would be had the white settlers been less intent on decimating and controlling the first people of North America and had endeavored, instead, to make relationships and to learn from them. What these early colonizers saw as simple and wild was, in fact, a complex and richly wise people whose thousands of years of living with this land garnered a knowledge that scientists still seek. You will know this by reading Ohiyesa's stories. Stories passed down for thousands of years. Stories of how to cauterize wounds with pine pitch by watching Mountain Lion. Where to best make a home, by observing where Elk makes her home. How to live in community like Beaver. It has taken hundreds of years for settlers to learn what Ohiyesa's people, and my own, have passed down in stories like these for thousands of years.

120 years after Ohiyesa's book was first published, populations of beings such as Grizzly and Mountain Lion have dwindled. Open, wild landscapes have been consumed by buildings, rivers dammed, and all of our lives threatened by a climate crisis; we return to these stories for a sense of hope, a chance to reconnect, to learn before it is too late.

In the following pages, the beings, along with the Indigenous people of the Dakota, offer us a teaching. An opportunity. You will undoubtedly notice several voices speaking to you from these pages. Human beings, yes, but also the animal beings. Animal beings are given agency here. And this matters. Perhaps in today's academic and literary world, giving voice to animals is childish and anthropocentric, but not so in Native stories and tradition. The wise, clever, loving, and fierce animal beings are seen as equals. They speak and are spoken of as kin. "We must remember," Ohiyesa writes, "that the four-footed people do not speak after our fashion. But what of that? Do we not talk with our eyes, lips, fingers? Love is made and murder done by the wink of an eye or by a single motion of the hand. Even we ourselves do not depend altogether upon speech for our communication with one another. Who can say that they have not a language?" Many might call this understanding of animal behavior and communication anthropomorphic, but I disagree. I believe that word comes from people who have forgotten who taught us, who showed us, and reflected for us who we are. We are not giving human traits to animal beings. We, all Indigenous people, for you are Indigenous to somewhere, too, watched the behavior of animals and land, used this as our mirror, learned and became who we are from close relationships and living with, not against or apart from, wildness.

"We Red men have no books nor do we build houses for schools, as the palefaces do. We are like the bear, the Beaver, the deer, who teach by example and action and experience," writes Ohiyesa. Watching them made us sly as foxes, clever as coyotes, and wise as owls. It was in this close observance that we learned to be, to hunt, to survive storms, and to live; we also knew to speak. The first languages were born of this relationship. We can see that in the Native words Ohiyesa offers in these stories. Look at the relationship between hō, which means yes and denotes approval, or a salutation, ho-yă´ which is a run of fish, and hō-yay which means "come on, let us do it." And most beautifully, Hō´-hay is the word used for Assiniboine people. Do you see the relationship? Not only between Hō and its livingness but, most notably, to the run of fish and the run of people in hō-yay. The Lakota language is said to date back to 900 CE. Then, stories were Images drawn on animal hides and later on fabric and paper. They were spoken then, and those who kept the stories were responsible for retelling the history to their community. Retelling in a language born of the landscape, a language and stories waiting for their teller or writer.

What you hold in your hands is a chance to connect with the knowledge that has always lived in this land. Not only to connect with the knowledge of Ohiyesa and his people but to reconnect with place. Reconnect with your ancestors, the ancestors of this place, the four-legged, the scaled, and the winged. In the preface, Ohiyesa writes, "And who is the grandfather of these silent people? Is it not the Great Mystery? For they know the laws of their life so well! They must have for their Maker our Maker. Then they are our brothers!"

What a different situation we might be in if we carried Ohiyesa's words with us. If we saw in Wolf and Grizzly, in rivers and trees, brothers and sisters. "In our stories, we find the medicine for understanding," writes Leslie Marmon Silko in her book *Ceremony*. Though I believe that Silko's understanding includes human's understanding one another, I think that she also means understanding of the nonhuman and of the land. Long before there were people with titles such as scientist, naturalists, biologist, and even writer, there were Native people whose attention, curiosity, and need for survival depended on knowing a place and its beings. That knowing created relationships, created language, created ceremony, and all became story. The stories in this collection are the words and relationships we have lost in the great gash created by colonialism. The stories in this collection are a lesson in paying attention, a class in writing from a nonhuman perspective, environmental and nature writing, and poetry. The stories gathered within these pages are medicine. Now that you have found them and they you, let them heal.

CMarie Fuhrman

AUTHOR'S NOTE

"And who is the grandfather of these silent people? Is it not the Great Mystery? For they know the laws of their life so well! They must have for their Maker our Maker. Then they are our brothers!"

Thus spoke one of the philosophers and orators of the Red men.

It is no wonder that the Indian held the animals to be his brothers. In his simple mind he regards the killing of certain of them for his sustenance to be an institution of the "Great Mystery." Therefore he kills them only as necessity and the exigencies of life demand, and not wantonly. He regards the spirit of the animal as a mystery belonging to the "Great Mystery," and very often after taking its life he pays due homage to its spirit. In many of the Dakota legends it appeared that such and such an animal came and offered itself as a sacrifice to save the Red man from starvation.

It was formerly held by him that the spirits of animals may communicate important messages to man. The wild hunter often refused during the remainder of his life to kill certain animals, after he had once become acquainted with their spirit or inner life. Many a hunter has absented himself for days and nights from his camp in pursuit of this knowledge. He considered it sacrilege to learn the secrets of an animal and then use this knowledge against him. If you wish to know his secrets you must show him that you are sincere, your spirit and his spirit must meet on common ground, and that is impossible until you have abandoned for the time being your habitation, your weapons, and all thoughts of the chase, and entered into perfect accord with the wild creatures. Such were some of the most sacred beliefs of the Red man, which led him to follow the trails of the animal people into seclusion and the wildest recesses of the woods and mountains.

Observations made for the purposes of the hunt are entirely distinct from this, the "spirit hunt," and include only the outward habits and noticeable actions of the game.

The stories contained in this book are based upon the common experiences and observations of the Red hunter. The main incidents in all of them, even those which are unusual and might appear incredible to the white man, are actually current among the Sioux and deemed by them worthy of belief.

When the life-story of an animal is given, the experiences described are typical and characteristic of its kind. Here and there the fables, songs, and superstitious fancies of the Indian are brought in to suggest his habit of mind and manner of regarding the four-footed tribes.

The scene of the stories is laid in the great Northwest, the ancient home of the Dakota or Sioux nation, my people. The Great Pipestone Quarry, Eagle's Nest Butte, the Little Rosebud River, and all the other places described under their real names are real and familiar features of that country, which now lies mainly within the States of Minnesota and the Dakotas. The time is before 1870, when the buffalo and other large game still roamed the wilderness and the Red men lived the life I knew as a boy.

Ohiyesa (Charles A. Eastman)
Amerst, Mass.

THE GREAT CAT'S NURSERY

A harsh and hateful cry of a sudden broke the peace of a midsummer night upon the creek called Bear-runs-in-the-Lodge. It told many things to the Red hunter, who, though the hour was late, still sat beside the dying camp-fire, pulling away at his long-stemmed pipe.

"Ugh!" he muttered, as he turned his head in the direction of the deep woods and listened attentively. The great cat's scream was not repeated. The hunter resumed his former attitude and continued to smoke.

The night was sultry and threatened storm, and all creatures, especially the fiercer wild animals, become nervous and irritable when thunder is in the air. Yet this fact did not fully explain to his mind Igmutanka's woman-like, almost hysterical complaint.

Having finished his smoke, he emptied the ashes out of the bowl of the pipe and laid it against the teepee-pole

1

at his back. "Ugh!" the hunter once more muttered to himself, this time with a certain complacency. "I will find your little ones to-morrow! That is what you fear."

The Bear-runs-in-the-Lodge is a deep and winding stream, a tributary of the Smoking Earth River, away up at the southern end of the Bad Lands. It is, or was then, an ideal home of wild game, and a resort for the wild hunters, both four-footed and human. Just here the stream, dammed of many beaver, widens its timbered bottoms, while its high banks and the rough country beyond are studded with dwarf pines and gullied here and there with cañon-like dry creeks.

Here the silvertip held supreme sway over all animals, barring an occasional contest with the mountain lion and with the buffalo bull upon the adjoining plains. It is true that these two were as often victorious as he of the big claws and sharp incisors, yet he remained the terror of that region, for he alone takes every opportunity to fight and is reckless in his courage, while other chiefs of the Wild Land prefer to avoid unnecessary trouble.

Igmutanka, the puma mother, had taken her leave of her two little tawny babes about the middle of the after-noon. The last bone of the buffalo calf which she had brought home from her last hunt had been served for dinner. Polished clean by her sharp teeth, it lay in the den for the kittens to play with. Her mate had left her early on that former hunt, and had not returned. She was very nervous about it, for already she feared the worst.

Since she came to Bear-runs they had been together,

and their chance acquaintance had become a love affair, and finally they had chosen and made a home for themselves. That was a home indeed! Wildness, mystery, and beauty combined in its outlook and satisfied every craving of the savage pair. They could scarcely say that it was quiet; for while they were unassuming enough and willing to mind their own affairs, Wild Land is always noisy, and the hubbub of the wild people quite as great in its way as that of the city of man.

The stream was dammed so often that Igmu did not have to jump it. The water-worn cliffs, arching and overhanging every turn of the creek, were dark with pines and cedars. Since her babies came she had not ventured upon any long hunts, although ordinarily she was the more successful of the two.

Now Igtin was gone and she was very hungry. She must go out to get meat. So, after admonishing her babies to be still during her absence, and not to come out of their den when Shunktokecha, the wolf, should invite them to do so, she went away.

As the great cat slunk down the valley of the Bear-runs she stopped and glanced nervously at every tree-root and grinning ledge of rock. On the way to Blacktail Creek she had to cross the divide, and when she had attained the Porcupine Butte she paused a moment for a survey, and saw a large herd of buffalo lying down. But their position was not convenient for an attack. There was no meat for her there.

She entered the upper end of the Blacktail and began

3

to hunt down to its mouth. At the first gulch there was a fresh trail. On that very morning three black-tail deer had watered there.

Igmu withdrew and re-entered the valley lower down. She took her stand upon a projection of the bank almost overhanging the stream, a group of buffalo-berry bushes partly concealing her position. Here they will pass, she thought, in returning to the main stream. Her calculation proved correct. Soon she saw a doe with two yearlings coming towards her, leisurely grazing on the choice grass.

The three were wholly unconscious of their danger. Igmu flattened her long, lanky body against the ground— her long, snaky tail slowly moved to and fro as the animals approached. In another moment she had sprung upon the nearest fawn! A shrill scream of agony and the cracking of tender bones mingled with the gladness of satisfying the pangs of hunger. The mother doe and the remaining fawn fled for their lives over the hills to the next creek, knowing well that she would not expose herself in an open chase.

She stood over the lifeless body for a moment, then grabbed it by the neck and dragged it into the dry bed of a small creek, where she was not likely to be disturbed at her feast. The venison tasted delicious, especially as the poor nursing mother was almost famished. Having eaten all she wanted, she put her claim-mark on the deer and covered it partly up. It was her practice to cover her game to season, and also to make it plain to all that know the laws of Wild Land that it is her game—Igmutanka's!

If any one disturbs it, he is running great risk of a pitched battle, for nothing exasperates her family like the theft of their game.

She could not carry any of it home with her, for even while she feasted she had seen an enemy pass by on the other side of the creek. He rode a long-tailed elk (pony) and carried a bagful of those dreadful winged willows, and the crooked stick which makes the winged willows fly. Igmu stopped eating at once and crouched lower. "Don't you dare come near me," was the thought apparent through her large, round eyes. The man passed without discovering her retreat.

"My babies!" thought Igmu. "They are all alone!" The mother-anxiety seized her. It was dangerous now to cross the open, but her desire to get back to her babies was stronger than fear. She ran up the ravine as far as it went; then, seeing no one, ran like a streak over the divide to the Porcupine Butte, where there were large rocks piled one upon another. Here she watched again under cover. "Aw-yaw-yaw!" burst from her in spite of herself. There were many cone-shaped teepees, which had sprung up since the day before upon the wide plain.

"There are the homes of those dreadful wild men! They always have with them many dogs, and these will surely find my home and babies," she thought. Although her anxiety was now very great, and the desire to reach home almost desperate, she yet kept her animal coolness and caution. She took a winding ravine which brought her nearer to Bear-runs, and now and then she had to run swiftly across the openings to gain less-exposed points.

At last she came to the old stream, and the crossing where the Bobtail Beaver had lived for as long as she knew anything about that country. Her dam was always in perfect order, and afforded an excellent bridge. To be sure, they had never been exactly on calling terms, but they had become accustomed to one another as neighbors, and especially whenever danger threatened upon the Bear-runs there was a certain sense of security and satisfaction to each in the presence of the other.

As she passed hurriedly over the dam she observed a trap. Igmu shivered as she recognized the article, and on a closer examination she detected the hated odor of man. She caught the string attached to it and jerked it out upon dry land, thus doing a good turn to her neighbor Sinteksa.

This discovery fully convinced her of the danger to her home and children. She picked her way through the deep woods, occasionally pausing to listen. At that time of the day no people talk except the winged people, and they were joyous as she passed through the timber. She heard the rushing of a water-fall over the cliff, now vibrating louder, now fainter as she listened. Far beyond, towards the wild men's camp, she heard the barking of a dog, which gave her a peculiar shiver of disgust.

A secret path led along the face of the cliff, and there was one open spot which she must cross to get to her den.

"Phur-r-r!" she breathed, and dropped to the ground. There stood one of the dreaded wild men!

No sooner had she put her head out of the woods than his quick eye caught her. "Igmutanka!" he exclaimed, and pulled one of the winged sticks out of his little bag.

Igmu was surprised for once, and fear almost overcame her. The danger to her children and the possible fate of her mate came into her mind in a flash. She hesitated for one instant, and in that instant she felt the sting of the swift arrow. She now ran for her life, and in another moment was out of sight among the gray ledges. "Ugh! I got her," muttered the Indian, as he examined the spot where she had stood.

Igmu never stopped until she reached her den. Her wild eyes gleamed as she paused at the entrance to ascertain whether any one had been there since she went away. When she saw and smelled that her home had not been visited, she forgot for the moment all her fright and pain. Her heart beat fast with joy—the mother-joy. Hastily she crawled into the dark cave.

"Yaw-aw-aw!" was the mother's greeting to her tawny babes. "Yaw-aw-aw!" they replied in chorus. She immediately laid herself down in the farthest corner of the den facing the entrance and invited her babies to come and partake of their food. Doubtless she was considering what she should do when the little ones had appeased their hunger.

Presently the bigger baby finished his meal and began

7

to claw the eyes of his brother. The latter pulled away, smacking his lips and blindly showing fight.

"Hush!" said the mother Igmu. "You must be good. Lie down and I will come back soon."

She came out of her den, still carrying the winged stick in her back. It was only a skin wound. She got hold of the end between her teeth and with one jerk she pulled it out. The blood flowed freely. She first rolled upon some loose earth and licked the wound thoroughly. After this she went and rubbed against pine pitch. Again she licked the pitch off from her fur; and having applied all the remedies known to her family, she re-entered the cave.

Igmu had decided to carry her helpless babes to a den she knew of upon Cedar Creek, near the old Eagle's Nest—a rough and remote spot where she felt sure that the wild men would not follow. But it was a long way to travel, and she could carry only one at a time. Meanwhile the hunters and their dogs would certainly track her to her den.

In her own mind she had considered the problem and hit upon an expedient. She took the smaller kitten by the skin of the back and hurried with it to her neighbor Sinteksa's place, down on the creek. There were some old, tumble-down beaver houses which had long been deserted. Without ceremony she entered one of these and made a temporary bed for her babe. Then she went back to her old home for the last time, took the other kitten in her mouth, and set out on her night journey to Cedar Creek.

It was now dark. Her shortest road led her near the camp of the red people; and as she knew that men and dogs seldom hunt by night, she ventured upon this way. Fires were blazing in the camp and the Red men were dancing the "coyote dance." It was a horrible din! Igmu trembled with fear and disgust as the odor of man came to her sensitive nostrils. It seemed to her at this moment that Igtin had certainly met his death at the hands of these dreadful people.

She trotted on as fast as she could with her load, only stopping now and then to put it down and lick the kitten's back. She laid her course straight over the divide, down to the creek, and then up towards its source. Here, in a wild and broken land, she knew of a cavern among piled-up rocks that she intended to make her own. She stopped at the concealed threshold, and, after satisfying herself that it was just as she had left it several months before, she prepared a bed within for her baby, and, having fed him, she admonished him to be quiet and left him alone. She must return at once for the other little cat.

But Igmu had gone through a great deal since the day before. It was now almost morning, and she was in need of food. She remembered the cached deer on the Blacktail Creek, and set out at once in that direction. As usual, there were many fresh deer-tracks, which, with the instinct of a hunter, she paused to examine, half inclined to follow them, but a second thought apparently impelled her to hurry on to her cache.

The day had now dawned and things appeared plain. She followed the creek-bed all the way to the spot where she had killed her deer on the day before. As she neared it her hunger became more and more irresistible; yet, instead of rushing upon her own, when she came within a few paces of it she stopped and laid herself prone upon the earth, according to the custom of her people. She could not see it, for it was hidden in a deep gully, the old bed of a dry stream. As she lay there she switched her tail slowly to and fro, and her eyes shot yellow fire.

Suddenly Igmu flattened out like a sunfish and began to whine nervously. Her eyes became two flaming globes of wrath and consternation. She gradually drew her whole body into a tense lump of muscles, ready to spring. Her lips unconsciously contracted, showing a set of fine teeth—her weapons—while the very ground upon which she lay was deeply scarred by those other weapons, the claws. Eagerly she listened once more—she could hear the cracking of bones under strong teeth.

Her blood now surged beyond all discretion and control. She thought of nothing but that the thief, whoever he might be, must feel the punishment due to his trespass. Two long springs, and she was on top of a wicked and huge grizzly, who was feasting on Igmutan-ka's cached deer! He had finished most of the tender meat, and had begun to clean his teeth by chewing some of the cartilaginous bones when the attack came.

"Waw-waw-waw-waaw!" yelled the old root-digger, and threw his immense left arm over his shoulder in an effort to seize his assailant. At the same time her weight and the force of her attack knocked him completely over and rolled him upon the sandy ground.

Igmu saw her chance and did not forget the usage of her people in a fight with his. She quickly sprang aside when she found that she could not hold her position, and there was danger of Mato slashing her side with either paw. She purposely threw herself upon her back, which position must have been pleasing to Mato, for he rushed upon her with all the confidence in the world, being ignorant of the trick.

It was not long before the old bear was forced to growl and howl unmercifully. He found that he could neither get in his best fight for himself nor get away from such a deadly and wily foe. He had hoped to chew her up in two winks, but this was a fatal mistake. She had sprung from the ground under him and had hugged him tight by burying the immense claws of her fore-paws in his hump, while her hind claws tore his loins and entrails. Thus he was left only his teeth to fight with; but even this was impossible, for she had pulled herself up close to his neck.

When Mato discovered his error he struggled desperately to get away, but his assailant would not let go her vantage-hold.

"Waw-waw-waw!" yelled the great boastful Mato once more, but this time the tone was that of weakness and defeat. It was a cry of "Murder! murder! Help! help!"

At last Igmutanka sprang aside, apparently to see how near dead the thief might be, and stood lashing her long, snaky tail indignantly.

"Waw-waw, yaw-waw!" moaned and groaned the grizzly, as he dragged himself away from the scene of the encounter. His wounds were deadly and ugly. He lay down within sight of the spot, for he could go no farther. He moaned and groaned more and more faintly; then he was silent. The great fighter and victor in many battles is dead!

Five paces from the remains of the cached deer the victor, lying in the shade of an immense pine, rested and licked her blood-soaked hair. She had received many ugly gashes, but none of them necessarily mortal. Again she applied her soil and pitch-pine remedy and stopped the hemorrhage. Having done this, she realized that she was still very hungry; but Igmu could not under any circumstances eat of the meat left and polluted by the thief. She could not break the custom of her people.

So she went across from Blacktail to the nearest point upon Bear-runs-in-the-Lodge, her former home, hoping to find some game on the way. As she followed the ravine leading from the creek of her fight she came upon a doe and fawn. She crouched down and crawled up close to them, then jumped upon the fawn. The luscious meat— she had all she wanted!

The day was now well advanced, and the harassed mother was growing impatient to reach the babe which she had left in one of the abandoned homes of Mrs. Bobtail Beaver. The trip over the divide between Black-tail and Bear-runs was quickly made. Fear, loneliness, and anxiety preyed upon her mind, and her body was weakened by loss of blood and severe exertion. She dwelt continually on her two babes, so far apart, and her dread lest the wild men should get one or both of them.

If Igmu had only known it, but one kitten was left to her at that moment! She had not left the cave on Cedar Creek more than a few minutes when her own cousin, whom she had never seen and who lived near the Eagle's Nest upon the same creek, came out for a hunt. She intercepted her track and followed it.

When she got to the den it was clear to Nakpaksa (Torn Ear) that this was not a regular home, so that she had a right to enter and investigate. To her surprise she found a little Igmutanka baby, and he cried when he saw her and seemed to be hungry. He was the age of her own baby which she had left not long before, and upon second thought she was not sure but that he was her own and that he had been stolen. He had evidently not been there long, and there was no one near to claim him. So she took him home with her. There she found her own kitten safe and glad to have a playmate, and Nakpaksa decided, untroubled by any pangs of conscience, to keep him and bring him up as her own.

It is clear that had Igmu returned and missed her baby there would have been trouble in the family. But, as the event proved, the cousin had really done a good deed.

It was sad but unavoidable that Igmu should pass near her old home in returning for the other kitten. When she crawled along the rocky ledge, in full view of the den, she wanted to stop. Yet she could not re-enter the home from which she had been forced to flee. It was not the custom of her people to do so. The home which they vacate by chance they may re-enter and even re-occupy, but never the home which they are forced to leave. There are evil spirits there!

Hurt and wearied, yet with courage unshaken, the poor savage mother glided along the stream. She saw Mrs. Bobtail and her old man cutting wood dangerously far from the water, but she could not stop and warn them because she had borrowed one of their deserted houses without their permission.

"Mur-r-r-r!" What is this she hears? It is the voice of the wild men's coyotes! It comes from the direction of the kitten's hiding-place. Off she went, only pausing once or twice to listen; but it became more and more clear that there was yelling of the wild men as well.

She now ran along the high ledges, concealing herself behind trees and rocks, until she came to a point from which she could overlook the scene. Quickly and stealthily she climbed a large pine. Behold, the little Igmu was up a small willow-tree! Three Indians were trying to shake him down, and their dogs were hilarious over the fun.

Her eyes flamed once more with wrath and rebellion against injustice. Could neither man nor beast respect her rights? It was horrible! Down she came, and with swift and cautious step advanced within a very few paces of the tree before man or beast suspected her approach.

Just then they shook the tree vigorously, while the poor little Igmu, clinging to the bough, yelled out pitifully, "Waw, waw, waw!"

Mother-love and madness now raged in her bosom. She could not be quiet any longer! One or two long springs brought her to the tree. The black coyotes and the wild men were surprised and fled for their lives.

Igmu seized and tore the side of one of the men, and threw a dog against the rocks with a broken leg. Then in lightning fashion she ran up the tree to rescue her kitten, and sprang to the ground, carrying it in her teeth. As the terrified hunters scattered from the tree, she chose the path along the creek bottom for her flight.

Just as she thought she had cleared the danger-point a wild man appeared upon the bank overhead and, quick as a flash, sent one of those winged willows. She felt a sharp pang in her side—a faintness—she could not run! The little Igmu for whom she had made such a noble fight dropped from her mouth. She staggered towards the bank, but her strength refused her, so she lay down beside a large rock. The baby came to her immediately, for he had not had any milk since the day before. She gave one gentle lick to his woolly head before she dropped her own and died.

"Woo, woo! Igmutanka ye lo! Woo, woo!" the shout of triumph resounded from the cliffs of Bear-runs-in-the-Lodge. The successful hunter took home with him the last of the Igmu family, the little orphaned kitten.

ON WOLF MOUNTAIN

O n the eastern slope of the Big Horn Mountains, the Mayala clan of gray wolves, they of the Steep Places, were following on the trail of a herd of elk. It was a day in late autumn. The sun had appeared for an instant, and then passed behind a bank of cold cloud. Big flakes of snow were coming down, as the lean, gray hunters threaded a long ravine, cautiously stopping at every knoll or divide to survey the outlook before continuing their uncertain pursuit.

The large Mayala wolf with his mate and their five full-grown pups had been driven away from their den on account of their depredations upon the only paleface in the Big Horn valley. It is true that, from their stand-point, he had no right to encroach upon their hunting-grounds.

For three days they had been trailing over the Big Horn Mountains, moving southeast towards Tongue

River, where they believed that no man would come to disturb them. They had passed through a country full of game, but, being conscious of the pursuit of the sheepman and his party on their trail, they had not ventured to make an open hunt, nor were they stopping anywhere long enough to seek big game with success. Only an occasional rabbit or grouse had furnished them with a scanty meal.

From the Black Cañon, the outlet of the Big Horn River, there unfolds a beautiful valley. Here the wild man's ponies were scattered all along the river-bottoms. In a sheltered spot his egg-shaped teepees were ranged in circular form. The Mayala family deliberately sat upon their haunches at the head of the cañon and watched the people moving, antlike, among the lodges.

Manitoo, the largest of the five pups, was a famous runner and hunter already. He whimpered at sight of the frail homes of the wild man, and would fain have gotten to the gulches again.

The old wolf rebuked his timidity with a low growl. He had hunted many a time with one of these Red hunters as guide and companion. More than this, he knew that they often kill many buffalo and elk in one hunting, and leave much meat upon the plains for the wolf people. They respect his medicine and he respects theirs. It is quite another kind of man who is their enemy.

Plainly there was an unusual commotion in the Sioux

village. Ponies were brought in, and presently all the men rode out in a southerly direction.

"Woo-o-o!" was the long howl of the old wolf. It sounded almost like a cry of joy.

"It is the buffalo-hunt! We must run to the south and watch until the hunt is ended."

Away they went, travelling in pairs and at some distance apart, for the sake of better precaution. On the south side of the mountain they stood in a row, watching hungrily the hunt of the Red men.

There was, indeed, a great herd of buffalo grazing upon the river plain surrounded by foot-hills. The hunters showed their heads on three sides of the herd, the fourth side rising abruptly to the sheer ascent of the mountain.

Now there arose in the distance a hoarse shout from hundreds of throats in unison. The trained ponies of the Indians charged upon the herd, just as the wolves themselves had sometimes banded together for the attack in better days of their people. It was not greatly different from the first onset upon the enemy in battle. Yelling and brandishing their weapons, the Sioux converged upon the unsuspecting buffalo, who fled blindly in the only direction open to them—straight toward the inaccessible steep!

In a breath, men and shaggy beasts were mixed in struggling confusion. Many arrows sped to their mark and dead buffalo lay scattered over the plain like big, black mounds, while the panic-stricken survivors fled down the valley of the Big Horn. In a little while the successful hunters departed with as much meat as their ponies could carry.

No sooner were they out of sight than the old wolf gave a feast-call. "Woo-o-o! woo, woo, woo!" He was sure that they had left enough meat for all the wolf people within hearing distance. Then away they all went for the hunting-ground—not in regular order, as before, but each one running at his best speed. They had not gone far down the slope before they saw others coming from other hills—their gray tribesmen of the rocks and plains.

The Mayala family came first to two large cows killed near together. There is no doubt that they were hungry, but the smell of man offends all of the animal kind. They had to pause at a distance of a few paces, as if to make sure that there would be no trick played on them. The old Mayala chief knew that the man with hair on his face has many tricks. He has a black, iron ring that is hidden under earth or snow to entrap the wolf people, and some-times he puts medicine on the meat that tortures and kills them. Although they had seen these buffalo fall before their brothers, the wild Red men, they instinctively hesi-tated before taking the meat. But in the mean time there were others who came very hungry and who were, appar-ently, less scrupulous, for they immediately took hold of it, so that the Mayala people had to hurry to get their share.

In a short time all the meat left from the wild men's hunt had disappeared, and the wolves began grinding the soft and spongy portions of the bones. The old ones were satisfied and lay down, while the young ones, like young folks of any race, sat up pertly and gossiped or squabbled until it was time to go home.

Suddenly they all heard a distant call—a gathering call. "Woo-oo-oo!" After a few minutes it came again. Every gray wolf within hearing obeyed the summons without hesitation.

Away up in the secret recesses of the Big Horn Mountains they all came by tens and hundreds to the war-meeting of the wolves. The Mayala chief and his young warriors arrived at the spot in good season. Manitoo was eager to know the reason of this great council. He was young, and had never before seen such a gathering of his people.

A gaunt old wolf, with only one eye and an immensely long nose, occupied the place of honor. No human ear heard the speech of the chieftain, but we can guess what he had to say. Doubtless he spoke in defence of his country, the home of his race and that of the Red man, whom he regarded with toleration. It was altogether different with that hairy-faced man who had lately come among them to lay waste the forests and tear up the very earth about his dwelling, while his creatures devoured the herbage of the plain. It would not be strange if war were declared upon the intruder.

"Woo! woo! woo!" The word of assent came forth from the throats of all who heard the command at that wild council among the piled-up rocks, in the shivering dusk of a November evening.

The northeast wind came with a vengeance—every gust swayed and bent even the mighty pines of the mountains. Soon the land became white with snow. The air was full of biting cold, and there was an awfulness about the night.

The sheepman at his lonely ranch had little warning of the storm, and he did not get half of his cows in the corral. As for the sheep, he had already rounded them up before the blizzard set in.

"My steers, I reckon, 'll find plenty of warm places for shelter," he remarked to his man. "I kinder expect that some of my cows'll suffer; but the worst of it is the wolves—confound them! The brutes been howling last night and again this evenin' from pretty nigh every hill-top. They do say, too, as that's a sure sign of storm!"

The long log-cabin creaked dismally under the blast, and the windward windows were soon coated with snow.

"What's that, Jake? Sounds like a lamb bleating," the worried rancher continued.

Jake forcibly pushed open the rude door and listened attentively.

"There is some trouble at the sheep-sheds, but I can't tell just what 'tis. May be only the wind rattling the loose boards," he suggested, uncertainly.

"I expect a grizzly has got in among the sheep, but

I'll show him that he is at the wrong door," exclaimed Hank Simmons, with grim determination. "Get your rifle, Jake, and we'll teach whoever or whatever it may be that we are able to take care of our stock in night and storm as well as in fair weather!"

He pushed the door open and gazed out into the darkness in his turn, but he could not see a foot over the threshold. A terrific gust of wind carried a pall of snow into the farthest corner of the cabin. But Hank was a determined fellow, and not afraid of hardship. He would spend a night in the sod stable to watch the coming of a calf, rather than run even a small chance of losing it.

Both men got into their cowhide overcoats and pulled their caps well down over their ears. Rifle in hand, they proceeded towards the sheep-corral in single file, Jake carrying the lantern. The lambs were bleating frantically, and as they approached the premises they discovered that most of the sheep were outside.

"Keep your finger on the trigger, Jake! All the wolves in the Big Horn Mountains are here!" exclaimed Hank, who was a few paces in advance.

Had they been inexperienced men—but they were not. They were both men of nerve. "Bang! bang!" came from two rifles, through the frosty air and blinding snow.

But the voice of the guns did not have the demoralizing effect upon which they had counted. Their assailants scarcely heard the reports for the roar of the storm. Undaunted by the dim glow of the lantern, they banded together for a fresh attack. The growling, snarling, and gnashing of teeth of hundreds of great gray wolves at close quarters were enough to dismay even Hank Simmons, who had seen more than one Indian fight and hair-breadth adventure.

"Bang! bang!" they kept on firing off their pieces, now and then swinging the guns in front of them to stay the mad rush of the wild army. The lantern-light revealed the glitter of a hundred pairs of fierce eyes and shining rows of pointed teeth.

Hank noticed a lean, gray wolf with one eye and an immense head who was foremost in the attack. Almost abreast of him was a young wolf, whose great size and bristling hair gave him an air of ferocity.

"Hold hard, Jake, or they'll pick our bones yet!" Hank exclaimed, and the pair began to retreat. They found it all they could do to keep off the wolves, and the faithful collie who had fought beside them was caught and dragged into darkness. At last Hank pushed the door open and both men tumbled backward into the cabin.

"Shoot! shoot! They have got me!" yelled Jake. The other snatched a blazing ember from the mud chimney and struck the leading wolf dead partly within the hut.

"Gol darn them!" ejaculated Jake, as he scrambled to his feet. "That young wolf is a good one for fighting—he almost jerked my right leg off!"

"Well, I'll be darned, Jake, if they haven't taken one of your boots for a trophy," Hank remarked, as he wiped the sweat from his brows, after kicking out the dead wolf and securely barring the door. "This is the closest call I've had yet! I calculate to stand off the Injuns most any time, but these here wolves have no respect for my good rifle!"

Wazeyah, the god of storm, and the wild mob reigned outside the cabin, while the two pioneer stockmen barricaded themselves within, and with many curses left the sheep to their fate.

The attack had stampeded the flock so that they broke through the corral. What the assailants did not kill the storm destroyed. On the plateau in front of Mayaska the wolves gathered, bringing lambs, and here Manitoo put down Jake's heavy cowhide boot, for it was he who fought side by side with the one-eyed leader.

He was immediately surrounded by the others, who examined what he had brought. It was clear that Manitoo had distinguished himself, for he had stood by the leader until he fell, and secured, besides, the only trophy of the fight.

Now they all gave the last war-cry together. It was the greatest wolf-cry that had been heard for many years upon those mountains. Before daybreak, according to custom, the clans separated, believing that they had effectually destroyed the business of the hairy-faced intruder, and expecting by instant flight to elude his vengeance.

On the day before the attack upon the ranch, an Indian from the camp in the valley had been appointed to scout the mountains for game. He was a daring scout, and was already far up the side of the peak which overhung the

Black Cañon when he noticed the air growing heavy and turned his pony's head towards camp. He urged him on, but the pony was tired, and, suddenly, a blinding storm came sweeping over the mountainside.

The Indian did not attempt to guide his intelligent beast. He merely fastened the lariat securely to his saddle and followed behind on foot, holding to the animal's tail. He could not see, but soon he felt the pony lead him down a hill. At the bottom it was warm, and the wind did not blow much there. The Indian took the saddle off and placed it in a wash-out which was almost dry. He wrapped himself in his blanket and lay down. For a long time he could feel and hear the foot-falls of his pony just above him, but at last he fell asleep.

In the morning the sun shone and the wind had subsided. The scout started for camp, knowing only the general direction, but in his windings he came by accident upon the secret place, a sort of natural cave, where the wolves had held their war meeting. The signs of such a meeting were clear to him, and explained the unusual number of wolf-tracks which he had noticed in this region on the day before. Farther down was the plateau, or wopata, where he found the carcasses of many sheep, and there lay Jake's boot upon the bloody and trampled snow!

When he reached the camp and reported these signs to his people, they received the news with satisfaction.

"The paleface," said they, "has no rights in this region. It is against our interest to allow him to come here, and our brother of the wandering foot well knows it for a menace to his race. He has declared war upon the sheepman, and it is good. Let us sing war-songs for the success of our brother!" The Sioux immediately despatched runners to learn the exact state of affairs upon Hank Simmons's ranch.

In the mean time the ruined sheepman had made his way to the nearest army post, which stood upon a level plateau in front of Hog's Back Mountain.

"Hello, Hank, what's the matter now?" quoth the sutler. "You look uncommonly serious this morning. Are the Injuns on your trail again?"

"No, but it's worse this time. The gray wolves of the Big Horn Mountains attacked my place last night and pretty near wiped us out! Every sheep is dead. They even carried off Jake Hansen's boot, and he came within one of being eaten alive. We used up every cartridge in our belts, and the bloody brutes never noticed them no more than if they were pebbles! I'm afraid the post can't help me this time," he concluded, with a deep sigh.

"Oh, the devil! You don't mean it," exclaimed the other. "Well, I told you before to take out all the strychnine you could get hold of. We have got to rid the country of the Injuns and gray wolves before civilization will stick in this region!"

Manitoo had lost one of his brothers in the great fight, and another was badly hurt. When the war-party broke up, Manitoo lingered behind to look for his wounded brother. For the first day or two he would occasionally meet one of his relations, but as the clan started south-east towards Wolf Mountain, he was left far behind.

When he had found his brother lying helpless a little way from the last gathering of the wolf people, he licked much of the blood from his coat and urged him to rise and seek a safer place. The wounded gray with difficulty got upon his feet and followed at some distance, so that in case of danger the other could give the signal in time.

Manitoo ran nimbly along the side gulches until he found a small cave. "Here you may stay. I will go hunting," he said, as plain as signs can speak.

It was not difficult to find meat, and a part of Hank's mutton was brought to the cave. In the morning Manitoo got up early and stretched himself. His brother did not offer to move. At last he made a feeble motion with his head, opened his eyes and looked directly at him for a moment, then closed them for the last time. A tremor passed through the body of the warrior gray, and he was still. Manitoo touched his nose gently, but there was no breath there. It was time for him to go.

When he came out of the death-cave on Plum Creek, Manitoo struck out at once for the Wolf Mountain region. His instinct told him to seek a refuge as far as possible from the place of death. As he made his way over the divide he saw no recent sign of man or of his own kinsfolk. Nevertheless, he had lingered too long for safety. The soldiers at the post had come to the aid of the sheepman, and they were hot on his trail. Perhaps his senses were less alert than usual that morning, for when he discovered the truth it was almost too late.

A long line of hairy-faced men, riding big horses and armed with rifles, galloped down the valley.

"There goes one of the gray devils!" shouted a corporal.

In another breath the awful weapons talked over his head, and Manitoo was running at top speed through a hail of bullets. It was a chase to kill, and for him a run for his life. His only chance lay in reaching the bad places. He had but two hundred paces' start. Men and dogs were gaining on him when at last he struck a deep gulch. He dodged the men around the banks, and their dogs were not experts in that kind of country.

The Sioux runners in the mean time had appeared upon a neighboring butte, and the soldiers, taking them for a war-party, had given up the chase and returned to the post. So, perhaps, after all, his brothers, the wild hunters, had saved Manitoo's life.

During the next few days the young wolf proceeded with caution, and had finally crossed the divide without meeting either friend or foe. He was now, in truth, an outcast and a wanderer. He hunted as best he could with very little success, and grew leaner and hungrier than he had ever been before in his life. Winter was closing in with all its savage rigor, and again night and storm shut down over Wolf Mountain.

. . .

The tall pines on the hill-side sighed and moaned as a new gust of wind swept over them. The snow came faster and faster. Manitoo had now and again to change his position, where he stood huddled up under an overarching cliff. He shook and shook to free himself from the snow and icicles that clung to his long hair.

He had been following several black-tail deer into a gulch when the storm overtook him, and he sought out a spot which was somewhat protected from the wind. It was a steep place facing southward, well up on the side of Wolf Mountain.

Buffalo were plenty then, but as Manitoo was alone he had been unable to get meat. These great beasts are dangerous fighters when wounded, and unless he had some help it would be risking too much to tackle one openly. A band of wolves will attack a herd when very hungry, but as the buffalo then make a fence of themselves, the bulls facing outward, and keep the little ones inside, it is only by tiring them out and stampeding the herd that it is possible to secure one.

Still the wind blew and the snow fell fast. The pine-trees looked like wild men wrapped in their robes, and the larger ones might have passed for their cone-shaped lodges. Manitoo did not feel cold, but he was soon covered so completely that no eye of any of the wild tribes of that region could have distinguished him from a snow-clad rock or mound.

It is true that no good hunter of his tribe would willingly remain idle on such a day as that, for the prey is weakest and most easily conquered on a stormy day. But the long journey from his old home had somewhat disheartened Manitoo; he was weak from lack of food, and, more than all, depressed by a sense of his loneliness. He is as keen for the companionship of his kind as his brother the Indian, and now he longed with a great longing for a sight of the other members of the Mayala clan. Still he stood there motionless, only now and then sniffing the unsteady air, with the hope of discovering some passer-by.

Suddenly out of the gray fog and frost something emerged. Manitoo was hidden perfectly, but at that moment he detected with joy the smell of one of his own people. He sat up on his haunches awaiting the newcomer, and even gave a playful growl by way of friendly greeting.

The stranger stopped short as if frozen in her tracks, and Manitoo perceived a lovely maid of his tribe, robed in beautiful white snow over her gray coat. She understood the sign language of the handsome young man, with as nice a pair of eyes as she had ever seen in one of the wolf kind. She gave a yelp of glad surprise and sprang aside a pace or two.

Manitoo forgot his hunger and loneliness. He forgot even the hairy-faced men with the talking weapons. He lifted his splendid, bushy tail in a rollicking manner and stepped up to her. She raised her beautiful tail coquet-

31

tishly and again leaped sidewise with affected timidity.

Manitoo now threw his head back to sniff the wind, and all the hair of his back rose up in a perpendicular brush. Under other circumstances this would be construed as a sign of great irritation, but this time it indicated the height of joy.

The wild courtship was brief. Soon both were satisfied and stood face to face, both with plumy tail erect and cocked head. Manitoo teasingly raised one of his forepaws. They did not know how long they stood there, and no one else can tell. The storm troubled them not at all, and all at once they discovered that the sun was shining!

If any had chanced to be near the Antelope's Leap at that moment, he would have seen a beautiful sight. The cliff formed by the abrupt ending of a little gulch was laced with stately pines, all clad in a heavy garment of snow. They stood like shapes of beauty robed in white and jewels, all fired by the sudden bursting forth of the afternoon sun.

The wolf maiden was beautiful! Her robe was fringed with icicles which shone brilliantly as she stood there a bride. The last gust of wind was like the distant dying away of the wedding march, and the murmuring pines said Amen.

It was not heard by human ear, but according to the customs of the gray wolf clan it was then and there Manitoo promised to protect and hunt for his mate during their lifetime.

THE DANCE OF
THE LITTLE PEOPLE

I n full view of Wetaota, upon an open terrace half-
way up the side of the hill in the midst of virgin
Big Woods, there were grouped in an irregular
circle thirty teepees of the Sioux. The yellowish-white
skin cones contrasted quite naturally with the variegated
foliage of September, yet all of the woodland people
knew well that they had not been there on the day before.

Wetaota, the Lake of Many Islands, lies at the heart
of Haya Tanka, the Big Mountain. It is the chosen home
of many wild tribes. Here the crane, the Canadian goose,
the loon, and other water-fowl come annually to breed
undisturbed. The moose are indeed the great folk of the
woods, and yet there are many more who are happily
paired here, and who with equal right may claim it as
their domicile. Among them are some insignificant and
obscure, perhaps only because they have little or nothing
to contribute to the necessities of the wild man.

Such are the Little People of the Meadow, who dwell under a thatched roof of coarse grasses. Their hidden highways and cities are found near the lake and along the courses of the streams. Here they have toiled and played and brought forth countless generations, and few can tell their life-story.

"Ho, ho, kola!" was the shout of a sturdy Indian boy, apparently about ten years old, from his post in front of the camp and overlooking the lake. A second boy was coming towards him through the woods, chanting aloud a hunting song after the fashion of their fathers. The men had long since departed on the hunt, and Teola, who loved to explore new country, had already made the circuit of Wetaota. He had walked for miles along its tortuous sandy shores, and examined the signs of most of the inhabitants.

There were footprints of bears, moose, deer, wolves, mink, otter, and others. The sight of them had rejoiced the young hunter's heart, but he knew that they were for his elders. The woods were also full of squirrels, rabbits, and the smaller winged tribes, and the waters alive with the finny folk, all of which are boys' game. Yet it was the delicate sign-language of the Hetunkala, the Little People of the Meadow, which had aroused the enthusiasm of Teola, and in spite of himself he began to sing the game scout's song, when Shungela heard and gave him greeting.

"What is the prospect for our hunt to-day?" called Shungela, as soon as his friend was near enough to speak.

"Good!" Teola replied, simply. "It is a land of fatness. I have looked over the shores of Wetaota, and I think this is the finest country I have ever seen. I am tired enough of prairie-dog hunts and catching young prairie-chickens, but there is everything here that we can chase, kill, or eat."

Shungela at once circulated the good game news among the boys, and in less time than it takes an old man to tell a story all the boys of the camp had gathered around a bonfire in the woods.

"You, Teola, tell us again what you have seen," they exclaimed, in chorus.

"I saw the footprint of every creature that the Great Mystery has made! We can fish, we can hunt the young crane, and snare the rabbit. We can fool the owl for a night-play," he replied, proudly.

"Ho, kola, washtay! Good news! good news!" one urchin shouted. Another ran up a tree like a squirrel in the exuberance of his delight. "Heye, heye, he-e-e-e!" sang another, joyously.

"Most of all in number are the Little People of the Meadow! Countless are their tiny footprints on the sandy shores of Wetaota! Very many are their nests and furrows under the heavy grass of the marshes! Let Shungela be the leader to-day in our attack upon the villages of the Little People," suggested Teola, in whose mischievous

35

black eyes and shaggy mane one beheld the very picture of a wild rogue.

"Ho, ho, hechetu!" they all replied, in chorus.

"This is our first mouse-hunt this season, and you all know the custom. We must first make our tiny bows and arrows," he said, again.

"Tosh, tosh! Of course!" said they all.

In the late afternoon the sun shone warmly and everything was still in the woods, but upon the lake the occasional cry of the loon was heard. At some distance from the camp thirty or more little redskins met together to organize their mimic deer-hunt. They imitated closely the customs and manners of their elders while hunting the deer. Shungela gave the command, and all the boys advanced abreast, singing their hunting song, until they reached the meadow-land.

Here the leader divided them into two parties, of which one went twenty paces in advance, and with light switches raked aside the dead grass, exposing a net-work of trails. The homes of the Little People were under-ground, and the doors were concealed by last year's rank vegetation. While they kneeled ready to shoot with the miniature bow and arrows the first fugitives that might pass, the second party advanced in turn, giving an imitation of the fox-call to scare the timorous Little People. These soon became bewildered, missed their holes, and were shot down with unerring aim as they fled along their furrow-like paths.

There was a close rivalry among the boys to see who

could bring down the largest number of the tiny fugitives, but it was forbidden to open the homes or kill any who were in hiding.

In a few minutes the mice were panic-stricken, running blindly to and fro, and the excitement became general.

"Yehe, yehe! There goes their chief! A white mouse!" exclaimed one of the boys.

"Stop shooting!" came the imperative command from the shaggy-haired boy.

"It is a good sign to see their chief, but it is a very bad sign if we kill any after we have seen him," he explained.

"I have never heard that this is so," demurred Shun-gela, unwilling to yield his authority.

"You can ask your grandmother or your grandfather to-night, and you will find that I am right," retorted the shaggy-haired one.

"Woo, woo!" they called, and all the others came running.

"How many of you saw the white mouse?" Teola asked.

"I saw it!" "I too!" "I too!" replied several.

"And how many have heard that to see the chief of the mouse people brings good luck if the mice are spared after his appearance, but that whoever continues to kill them invites misfortune?"

"I have heard it!" "And I!" "And I!" The replies were so many that all the boys were willing to concede the authenticity of the story, and the hunt was stopped.

"Let us hear the mouse legends again this evening. My grandfather will tell them to us," Teola suggested, and not a boy there but was ready to accept the invitation.

Padanee was an ordinary looking old Indian, except that he had a really extraordinary pair of eyes, whose searching vision it seemed that nothing could escape. These eyes of his were well supported by an uncommonly good memory. His dusky and furrowed countenance was lighted as by an inner flame when once he had wound the buffalo-robe about his lean, brown limbs and entered upon the account of his day's experience in the chase, or prepared to relate to an attentive circle some oft-repeated tradition of his people.

"Hun, hun, hay!" The old savage cleared his throat. A crowd of bright-eyed little urchins had slipped quietly into his lodge. "Teola tells me that you had all set out to hunt down and destroy the Little People of the Meadow, and were only stopped by seeing their chief go by. I want to tell you something about the lives of these little creatures. We know that they are food for foxes and other animals, and that is as far as most of us think upon the matter. Yet the Great Mystery must have had some purpose in mind when He made them, and doubtless that is good for us to know."

Padanee was considered a very good savage schoolteacher, and he easily held his audience.

38

"When you make mud animals," he continued, "you are apt to vary them a little, perhaps for fun and perhaps only by accident. It is so with the Great Mystery. He seems to get tired of making all the animals alike, for in every tribe there are differences.

"Among the Hetunkala, the Little People, there are several different bands. Some live in one place and build towns and cities like the white man. Some wander much over forest and prairie, like our own people. These are very small, with long tails, and they are great jumpers. They are the thieves of their nation. They never put up any food of their own, but rob the store-houses of other tribes.

"Then there is the bobtailed mouse with white breast. He is very much like the paleface—always at work. He cannot pass by a field of the wild purple beans without stopping to dig up a few and tasting to see if they are of the right sort. These make their home upon the low-lying prairies, and fill their holes with great store of wild beans and edible roots, only to be robbed by the gopher, the skunk, the badger, who not only steal from them but often kill and eat the owner as well. Our old women, too, sometimes rob them of their wild beans.

"This fellow is always fat and well-fed, like the white man. He is a harvester, and his full store-houses are found all through the bottom lands."

"Ho, ho! Washtay lo!" the boys shouted. "Keep on, grandfather!"

"Perhaps you have heard, perhaps not," resumed the

old man. "But it is the truth. These little folk have their own ways. They have their plays and dances, like any other nation."

"We never heard it; or, if we have, we can remember it better if you will tell it to us again!" declared the shaggy-haired boy, with enthusiasm.

"Ho, ho, ho!" they all exclaimed, in chorus.

"Each full moon, the smallest of the mouse tribe, he of the very sharp nose and long tail, holds a great dance in an open field, or on a sandy shore, or upon the crusty snow. The dance is in honor of those who are to be cast down from the sky when the nibbling of the moon begins; for these Hetunkala are the Moon-Nibblers."

As this new idea dawned upon Padanee's listeners, all tightened their robes around them and sat up eagerly.

At this point a few powerful notes of a wild, melodious music burst spontaneously from the throat of the old teacher, for he was wont to strike up a song as a sort of interlude. He threw his massive head back, and his naked chest heaved up and down like a bellows.

"One of you must dance to this part, for the story is of a dance and feast!" he exclaimed, as he began the second stanza.

Teola instantly slipped out of his buffalo-robe and stepped into the centre of the circle, where he danced crouchingly in the firelight, keeping time with his lithe brown body to the rhythm of the legend-teller's song.

"O-o-o-o!" they all hooted at the finish.

"This is the legend of the Little People of the Meadow. Hear ye! Hear ye!" said Padanee.

"Ho-o-o!" was the instant response from the throats of the little Red men.

"A long time ago, the bear made a medicine feast, and invited the medicine-men (or priests) of all the tribes. Of each he asked one question, 'What is the best medicine (or magic) of your tribe?'

"All told except the little mouse. He was pressed for an answer, but replied, 'That is my secret.'

"Thereupon the bear was angry and jumped upon the mouse, who disappeared instantly. The big medicine-man blindly grabbed a handful of grass, hoping to squeeze him to death. But all the others present laughed and said, 'He is on your back!'

"Then the bear rolled upon the ground, but the mouse remained uppermost.

"'Ha, ha, ha!' laughed all the other medicine-men. 'You cannot get rid of him.'

"Then he begged them to knock him off, for he feared the mouse might run into his ear. But they all refused to interfere.

"'Try your magic on him,' said they, 'for he is only using the charm that was given him by the Great Mystery.'

"So the bear tried all his magic, but without effect. He had to promise the little mouse that, if he would only jump off from his body, neither he nor any of his tribe would ever again eat any of the Little People.

"Upon this the mouse jumped off.

"But now Hinhan, the owl, caught him between his awful talons, and said:

"'You must tell your charm to these people, or I will put my charm on you!'

"The little medicine-man trembled, and promised that he would if the owl would let him go. He was all alone and in their power, so at last he told it.

"'None of our medicine-men,' he began, 'dared to come to this lodge. I alone believed that you would treat me with the respect due to my profession, and I am here.' Upon this they all looked away, for they were ashamed.

"'I am one of the least of the Little People of the Meadow,' said the mouse. 'We were once a favored people, for we were born in the sky. We were able to ride the round moon as it rolls along. We were commissioned at every full moon to nibble off the bright surface little by little, until all was dark. After a time it was again silvered over by the Great Mystery, as a sign to the Earth People.

"'It happened that some of us were careless. We nibbled deeper than we ought, and made holes in the moon. For this we were hurled down to the earth. Many of us were killed; others fell upon soft ground and lived. We do not know how to work. We can only nibble other people's things and carry them away to our hiding-places. For this we are hated by all creatures, even by the working mice of our own nation. But we still retain our power to stay upon moving bodies, and that is our magic.'

"'Ho, ho, ho!' was the response of all present. They were obliged to respond thus, but they were angry with the little mouse, because he had shamed them.

"It was therefore decreed in that medicine-lodge that all the animals may kill the Hetunkala wherever they meet them, on the pretext that they do not belong upon earth. All do so to this day except the bear, who is obliged to keep his word."

"O-o-o-o!" shouted the shaggy-haired boy, who was rather a careless sort in his manners, for one should never interrupt a story-teller.

"It is almost full moon now, grandfather," he continued, "and there are nice, open, sandy places on the shore near the mouse villages. Do you think we might see them dancing if we should watch to-night?"

"Ho, takoja! Yes, my grandson," simply replied the old man.

The sand-bar in front of the Indian camp was at some little distance, out of hearing of the occasional loud laughter and singing of the people. Wetaota was studded with myriads of jewel-like sparkles. On the shadowy borders of the lake, tall trees bodied forth mysterious forms of darkness. There was something weird in all this beauty and silence.

The boys were scattered along in the tall grass near the sand-bar, which sloped down to the water's edge as smooth as a floor. All lay flat on their faces, rolled up in their warm buffalo-robes, and still further concealed by the shadows of the trees. The shaggy-haired boy had a bow and some of his best arrows hidden under his robe. No two boys were together, for they knew by experience the temptation to whisper under such circumstances. Every redskin was absorbed in watching for the Little People to appear upon their playground, and at the same time he must be upon the alert for an intruder, such as Red Fox, or the Hooting-owl of the woods.

"It seems strange," thought Teola, as he lay there motionless, facing the far-off silvery moon, "that these little folk should have been appointed to do a great work," for he had perfect faith in his grandfather's legend of the Moon-Nibblers.

"Ah-h-h!" he breathed, for now he heard a faint squeaking in the thick grass and rushes. Soon several tiny bodies appeared upon the open, sandy beach. They were so round and so tiny that one could scarcely detect the motion of their little feet. They ran to the edge of the water and others followed them, until there was a great mass of the Little People upon the clean, level sand.

"Oh, if Hinhan, the owl, should come now, he could carry away both claws full!" Teola fancied.

Presently there was a commotion among the Hetunkala, and many of them leaped high into the air, squeaking as if for a signal. Teola saw hundreds of mice coming from every direction. Some of them went close by his hiding-place, and they scrutinized his motionless body apparently with much care. But the young hunter instinctively held his breath, so that they could not smell him strongly, and at last all had gone by.

The big, brown mice did not attend this monthly carnival. They were too wise to expose themselves upon the open shore to the watchful eyes of their enemies. But upon the moonlit beach the small people, the Moon-Nibblers, had wholly given themselves up to enjoyment, and seemed to be forgetful of their danger. Here on Wetaota was the greatest gathering that Teola had ever seen in all his life.

Occasionally he thought he noticed the white mouse whom he supposed to be their chief, for no reason except that he was different from the others, and that was the superstition.

As he watched, circles were formed upon the sand, in which the mice ran round and round. At times they would all stand still, facing inward, while two or three leaped in and out of the ring with wonderful rapidity. There were many changes in the dance, and now and then one or two would remain motionless in the centre, apparently in performance of some ceremony which was not clear to Teola.

All at once the entire gathering became, in appearance, a heap of little round stones. There was neither sound nor motion.

"Ho, ho, ho!" Teola shouted, as he half raised himself from his hiding-place and flourished part of his robe in the clear moonlight. A big bird went up softly among the shadowy trees. All of the boys had been so fascinated by the dance that they had forgotten to watch for the coming of Hinhan, the owl, and now this sudden transformation of the Little People! Each one of them had rolled himself into the shape of a pebble, and sat motionless close to the sand to elude the big-eyed one.

They remained so until the owl had left his former perch and flown away to more auspicious hunting-grounds. Then the play and dance became more general and livelier than ever. The Moon-Nibblers were entirely given over to the spirit and gayety of the occasion. They ran in new circles, sometimes each biting the tail of his next neighbor. Again, after a great deal of squeaking, they all sprang high in the air, towards the calm, silvery orb of the moon. Apparently they also beheld it in front of them, reflected in the placid waters of Wetaota, for they advanced in columns to the water's edge, and there wheeled into circles and whirled in yet wilder dance.

At the height of the strange festival, another alarm came from the shaggy-haired boy. This time all the boys spied Red Fox coming as fast as his legs could carry him along the beach. He, too, had heard the fairy laughter and singing of the Moon-Nibblers, and never in his whole wild career is he better pleased than when he can catch a few of them for breakfast or supper.

No people know the secret of the dance except a few old Indians and Red Fox. He is so clever that he is always on the watch for it just before the full moon. At the first sound that came to his sharp ears he knew well what was going on, and the excitement was now so great that he was assured of a good supper.

"Hay-ahay! Hay-ahay!" shouted the shaggy-haired boy, and he sent a swift arrow on a dangerous mission for Red Fox. In a moment there came another war-whoop, and then another, and it was wisdom for the hungry one to take to the thick woods.

"Woo, woo! Eyaya lo! Woo, woo!" the boys shouted after him, but he was already lost in the shadows.

The boys came together. Not a single mouse was to be seen anywhere, nor would any one suspect that they had been there in such numbers a few moments earlier, except for the finest of tracery, like delicate handwriting, upon the moonlit sand.

"We have learned something to-night," said Teola. "It is good. As for me, I shall never again go out to hunt the Little People."

WECHAH THE PROVIDER

C ome, Wechah, come away! the dogs will tease you dreadfully if they find you up a tree. Enakanee (hurry)!" Wasula urged, but the mischievous Wechah still chose to remain upon the projecting limb of an oak which made him a comfortable seat. It was apparently a great temptation to him to climb every large, spreading tree that came in his way, and Wasula had had some thrilling experiences with her pet when he had been attacked by the dogs of the camp and even by wild animals, so it was no wonder that she felt some anxiety for him.

Wasula was the daughter of a well-known warrior of the Rock Cliff villagers of the Minnesota River. Her father had no son living, therefore she was an only child, and the most-sought-after of any maiden in that band. No other girl could boast of Wasula's skill in paddling the birch canoe or running upon snow-shoes, nor could any gather the wild rice faster than she. She could pitch the prettiest teepees, and her nimble, small fingers worked very skilfully with the needle. She had made many embroidered tobacco-pouches and quivers which the young men were eager to get.

More than all this, Wasula loved to roam alone in the woods. She was passionately fond of animals, so it was not strange that, when her father found and brought home a baby raccoon, the maiden took it for her own, kept it in an upright Indian cradle and played mother to it.

Wasula was as pretty and free as a teal-duck, or a mink with its slender, graceful body and small face. She had black, glossy hair, hanging in two plaits on each side of her head, and a calm, childlike face, with a delicate aquiline nose. Wechah, when he was first put into her hands, was nothing more than a tiny ball of striped fur, not unlike a little kitten. His bright eyes already shone with some suggestion of the mischief and cunning of his people. Wasula made a perfect baby of him. She even carved all sorts of playthings out of hoof and bone, and tied them to the bow of the cradle, and he loved to play with them. He apparently understood much that she said to him, but he never made any attempt to speak. He preferred to use what there is of his own language, but that, too, he kept from her as well as he could, for it is a secret belonging only to his tribe.

Wechah had now grown large and handsome, for he was fat and sleek. They had been constantly together for over a year, and his foster-mother had grown very much attached to him. The young men who courted Wasula had conspired at different times against his life, but upon second thought they realized that if Wasula should suspect the guilt of one of them his chance of winning her would be lost forever.

It is true he tried their patience severely, but he could not help this, for he loved his mistress, and his ambition was to be first in her regard. He was very jealous, and, if any one appeared to divide her attention, he would immediately do something to break up the company. Sometimes he would resort to hiding the young man's quiver, bow, or tomahawk, if perchance he put it down. Again he would pull his long hair, but they could never catch him at this. He was quick and sly. Once he tripped a proud warrior so that he fell sprawling at the feet of Wasula. This was embarrassing, and he would never again lay himself open to such a mishap. At another time he pulled the loose blanket off the suitor, and left him naked. Sometimes he would pull the eagle feather from the head of one and run up a tree with it, where he would remain, and no coaxing could induce him to come down until Wasula said:

"Wechah, give him his feather! He desires to go home."

Wechah truly thought this was bright and cunning, and Wasula thought so too. While she always reprimanded him, she was inwardly grateful to him for breaking the monotony of courtship or rebuking the presumption of some unwelcome suitor.

"Come down, Wechah!" she called, again and again. He came part way at last, only to take his seat upon another limb, where he formed himself into a veritable muff or nest upon the bough in a most unconcerned way. Any one else would have been so exasperated that all the dogs within hearing would have been called into service to bay him down, but Wasula's love for Wechah was truly strong, and her patience with him was extraordinary. At last she struck the tree a sharp blow with her hatchet. The little fellow picked himself up and hastily descended, for he knew that his mistress was in earnest, and she had a way of punishing him for disobedience. It was simple, but it was sufficient for Wechah.

Wasula had the skin of a buffalo calf's head for a work-bag, beautifully embroidered with porcupine quills about the open mouth, nose, eyes, and ears. She would slip this over Wechah's head and tie his fore-paws together so that he could not pull it off. Then she would take him to the spring under the shadow of the trees and let him look at himself. This was enough punishment for him. Sometimes even the mention of the calf's head was enough to make him submit.

Of course, the little Striped Face could take his leave at any time that he became dissatisfied with his life among the Red people. Wasula had made it plain to him that he was free. He could go or stay; but, apparently, he loved her too well to think of leaving. He would curl himself up into a ball and lie by the hour upon some convenient branch while the girl was cutting wood or sitting under a tree doing her needle-work. He would study her every movement, and very often divine her intentions.

Wasula was a friend to all the little people of the woods, and especially sympathized with the birds in their love-making and home-building. Wechah must learn to respect her wishes. He had once stolen and devoured some young robins. The parent birds were frantic about their loss, which attracted the girl's attention. The wicked animal was in the midst of his feast.

"Glechu! glechu (Come down)!" she called, excitedly. He fully understood from the tone that all was not right, but he would not jump from the tree and run for the deep woods, thereby avoiding punishment and gaining his freedom. The rogue came down with all the outward appearance of one who pleads guilty to the charge and throws himself upon the judge's mercy. She at once put him in the calf's head and bound his legs, and he had nothing to eat for a day and a night.

It was a great trial to both of them. Wadetaka, the dog, for whom he had no special love, was made to stand guard over the prisoner so that he could not get away and no other dog could take advantage of his helplessness. Wasula was very sorry for him, but she felt that he must learn his lesson. That night she lay awake for a long time. To be sure, Wechah had been good and quiet all day, but his tricks were many, and she had discovered that his people have danger-calls and calls for help quite different from their hunting and love calls.

After everybody was asleep, even Wadetaka apparently snoring, and the camp-fire was burning low, there was a gentle movement from the calf's-head bag. Wasula uncovered her head and listened. Wechah called softly for help.

"Poor Wechah! I don't want him to be angry with me, but he must let the little birds' homes alone."

Again Wechah gave his doleful call. In a little while she heard a stealthy footfall, and at the same time Wadetaka awoke and rushed upon something.

It was a large raccoon! He ran up a near-by tree to save himself, for Wadetaka had started all the dogs of the camp. Next the hunters came out. Wasula hurriedly put on her moccasins and ran to keep the men from shooting the rescuer.

Wechah's friend took up his position upon one of the upper limbs of a large oak, from which he looked down with blazing eyes upon a motley crew. Near the root of the tree Wechah lay curled up in a helpless ball. The new-comer scarcely understood how this unfortunate member of his tribe came into such a predicament, for when some one brought a torch he was seen to rise, but immediately fell over again.

"Please do not kill him," pleaded Wasula. "It is a visitor of my pet, whom I am punishing for his misconduct. As you know, he called for help according to the custom of his tribe."

They all laughed heartily, and each Indian tied up his dog for the rest of the night, so that the visitor might get away in safety, while the girl brought her pet to her own bed.

It was the Moon of Falling Leaves, and the band to which Wasula's father belonged were hunting in the deep woods in Minnesota, the Land of Sky-colored Water. The band had divided itself into many small parties for the fall and winter hunt. When this particular party reached Minnetonka, the Big Lake, they found the hunting excellent. Deer were plenty, and the many wooded islands afforded them good feeding-places. The men hunted daily, and the women were busy preparing the skins and curing the meat. Wechah wandered much alone, as Wasula was busy helping her mother.

All went well for many weeks; and even when the snow fell continuously for many a day and the wind began to blow, so that no hunter dared emerge from his teepee, there was dried venison still and all were cheerful. At last the sun appeared. "Hoye! hoye!" was the cheerful cry of the hunting bonfire-builder, very early in the morning. As it rang musically on the clear, frosty air, each hunter set out, carrying his snow-shoes upon his back, in the pleasant anticipation of a good hunt. After the customary smoke, they all disappeared in the woods on the north shore of Minnetonka.

Alas! it was a day of evil fortune. There was no warning. In the late afternoon one came back bleeding, singing a death-dirge. "We were attacked by the Ojib-ways! All are dead save myself!"

Thus was the little camp suddenly plunged into deep sorrow and mourning. Doleful wails came forth from every lodge, and the echoes from the many coves answered them with a double sadness.

Again the storm-wind raged. This time the dried meat was gone, and all the women did nothing but bewail their misfortunes. "The evil spirit is upon us!" they cried. "The enemy has taken away our husbands, and now Wazeyah, the god of storm and winter, is ready to slay us!" So they mourned as those having no hope.

When at last the storm ceased, the snow was very deep. The little ones were famished. There was no meat in the camp and there were no hunters to hunt. They were far from their permanent village upon the Minnesota River. They must have food first, and then try to get back. So, for the children's sake, the brave mothers and elder sisters began to look about them to decide upon some action.

"Wasula, my child, what are you thinking of?" the mother asked.

"Mother, my father taught me to hunt, and he took so much pride in my snow-shoeing! See, mother, here is one of his quivers full of arrows, and here is a good bow." The girl spoke earnestly. "I can take care of you, mother, until we get back to our relatives. I can shoot as straight as any brave, and my father taught me how to circle a doe or buck to a stand-still. Wechah will go with me and guide me, so that I shall not be lost," continued Wasula, with a show of cheerfulness.

"But you must be careful, my child! The Ojibways are not far away. Some of their warriors will perhaps have a mind to come again, now that they have overcome all the men of our little band," sadly warned the mother.

Meanwhile Wechah sat by watching every motion, as if trying to read their thoughts. He was evidently delighted when Wasula girdled herself and threw her snow-shoes diagonally across her back. He gave one big, joyous leap and ran out of sight ahead of her as she set out on the hunt. Her poor mother watched her through the pin-holes in the teepee. "Ah, I fear—I fear the dreadful warriors of the Ojibways!" she muttered.

They went over the snow-clad Minnetonka towards Crane Island, and the famished girl was scarcely able to run upon snow-shoes, although ordinarily it was an easy task for her. Her people had been living upon rose-berries and roots. Wechah, with a light foot, ran ahead of her into the thick woods.

No sooner was he out of sight of home than all his native cunning vividly returned to him, and the desire to find whatever was in his way. Through the frosty air and among the snow-clad multitudinous trees he swiftly ran. His ancient calling thrilled him through and through. Now and then he ran up a tree, leaped far into the soft snow, and away he glided again. Not yet do the wild inhabitants of the woods come out for their guest, at least not upon Crane Island, for Wechah had not crossed a single trail.

Deep in the forest at last the little Striped Face gave his signal-call, according to the custom of his people. Wasula turned in the direction of the sound and peered sharply through the snow-laden boughs. There he stood upon a large limb, anxiously awaiting her coming.

He leaped from his high perch toward her, struck the ground like a pillow, and made the soft snow fly up like loose feathers.

"I see—I see your deer-track," she laughed at him. "We shall try to get one! You must now follow me, Wechah. It is Wasula's turn to lead."

The maiden's bow was carefully examined, and she picked out one of her best arrows. Instead of following the trail, like a true hunter she started with the wind and ran along for some distance, then described a circle, coming just inside of her starting-point. Again she made another circle within the first, but no deer had crossed her track. Upon the third round she spied them hiding behind a large, fallen oak, whose dead leaves afforded some shelter. As she described another circle to get within arrow-shot, the doe stretched out at full length upon the snow, laying her ears back, rabbit-like, to escape detection. Wasula knew the trick of holding her. She did not pause for an instant, but ran along until she gained an opening for a shot. Then she turned quickly upon the quivering doe and let her swift arrow fly.

Instantly the doe and her two full-grown fawns got up

and sprang away through the woods and out of sight. Wasula had seen her arrow enter the doe's side. She examined the trail—it showed drops of blood—and immediately the huntress followed the trail.

In a few moments she heard Wechah give his shrill, weird 'coon-call. Through an alley between rows of trees she saw him standing proudly upon the dead body of Takcha.

"Oh, I thank thee, Great Mystery! I thank you, Wechah, for your kind guidance," Wasula spoke, in a trembling voice. She took her hunting-knife from her belt and skinned the legs of the doe up to the knee-joints. Having unjointed them, she drew the fore-legs backward and fastened them securely; then she put her hunting-strap through the under-jaw and attached her carrying-straps. Thus she proceeded to drag the body home.

Wechah was as happy as if he had shot the deer himself. Wasula realized that her people were starving and she ran as fast as she could, but before she was half-way across the lake her companion was in camp. As she approached the shore, the stronger of the women came running to meet and relieve her of her burden. They were overwhelmed with joy. She slipped off her shoulder-straps and ran to her mother, while two of the others hitched themselves to her carrying-lines and ran with the deer. "Wasula, heroine, huntress! The gracious and high-minded!" In such wise the old people sang her praises.

Several of the women had been out hunting, like Wasula, but none were as successful as she and Wechah had been. Some brought back a single rabbit or a grouse to quiet their crying babies. One brought a dead raccoon which she had found in a trap. Wasula was sorry when Wechah saw this and became visibly depressed.

When all the venison had been eaten, the rigor of winter still held in his northern clime. The maiden hunted every day, but without success. One afternoon the sun was getting low and she was still far from camp, but she could not bear to go back empty-handed. She felt that upon her success depended the lives of the others, for they could not yet move on foot toward the village on the Minnesota River—the children would suffer cruelly in such an attempt.

She was upon the trail of Shunktokecha, the wolf— not that she had any hope of overtaking him, but it is well known that he is a good guide. Wechah, too, was apparently unwilling to leave the trail. Their course was directed toward one of the outlets of the lake.

When they reached this stream, other trails joined the one they were following, making a broad path, and here and there the ice of the creek was scratched by the wolf people as they passed. The huntress quickened her steps in renewed hope. She knew that upon the trail there lies much of joy, of fascination, and catastrophe; but every trailer only keeps the joy in mind—it is enough to realize misfortune when it comes!

Around a sudden bend of the frozen creek another hunter's voice was heard. It was Kangee, the raven.

"Surely, there is game there, dead or alive, for Kangee never speaks without a cause," she murmured.

Now Wechah disappeared around the point, and when she came into full view she saw her pet jerk out of the stream something living. As the object fell it curved itself upon the ice and again sprang glittering in the air.

Wasula laughed, in spite of herself, the sing-song laugh of the wild maid of the woods. "Hoya! hoya!" she screamed, and ran forward. Again and again Wechah snatched out of the live water a large fish. When she reached the spring in the creek, her pet had already taken out enough to feed the whole camp.

The girl fell on her knees and peered into the water. It was packed to the ice with the spring exodus of the finny tribes of Minnetonka for the spawning! Every year, before the spring opens, they crowd upon one another in the narrow passes of the streams. There was a spring here where the ice was open, and hence the broad trail and the scratches of wolves, bears, raccoons, crows, ravens, and many more.

"Good Wechah! We shall live now—our people cannot starve," said Wasula, feelingly, to her pet. Her responsibility as the main support of the camp was greatly lightened. At last she took her hunting-knife from her belt and stripped the bark from a near-by birch. She shaped it into a rough canoe and threw into it as many fish as it would hold. The sun already hovered among the tree-tops as she hitched herself by means of her carrying-lines to the canoe-shaped tray full of fish and started homeward across an arm of the frozen lake.

Wechah ran playfully in front of her. The wild pet was full of his cunning ways. When they reached a wooded shore he suddenly disappeared, and the girl did not know which way he went. Presently she thought she heard a baby cry away off in the woods; in a little while there seemed to be a skunk calling, nearer, and still nearer; again she heard the call of an owl. Finally the mimic rushed upon her from behind the shadow of a huge pine, swiftly pursued by a bob-tailed 'coon.

"Ugh, Wechah! are you afraid of Sintay? 'Tis he is wicked and full of cunning! He has broken away from several steel traps, and he always takes the bait of a dead-fall without harm to himself. If he ever chases you again I will punish him," declared the huntress.

On seeing Wasula, the animal had disappeared among the shadows almost as mysteriously as he emerged from them. It was now the close of Wechah tawee, the 'coon's month, when the male raccoon leaves his winter quarters and begins to look for company. This particular individual was well known to the Indian hunters upon Lake Minnetonka. As Wasula had said, he was the cunningest of his tribe, and he was also unusually large and of a savage disposition. True, he fared luxuriously every day upon berries, mice, fish, frogs, eggs from the swamps, and young birds not yet able to fly. Then he sleeps a long and happy sleep through the coldest moons of the year, undisturbed save when the Red man and his dogs are about—he who loves to eat the fat of the 'coon and makes a beautiful robe of his striped skin!

"You must keep away from Sintay, for he is dangerous," said Wasula, who always talked to her pet as if he understood every word she said. Nevertheless, while she struggled on with her load he had once more disappeared. Soon a cry from him attracted her attention, and turning a little aside from her path, she beheld Sintay sitting upon a snow-covered log at the root of a large hollow tree, holding a comb of wild honey in his two paws, listening angrily and growling over his interrupted meal. In a moment something sprang into the air directly over his head and alighted in front of him. It was Wechah.

Sintay screamed and clawed the air with his right paw, at the same time clinging to the comb with the left. The new-comer bravely faced him. Both were desperately in earnest, growling and snapping their sharp teeth. The bee-tree was the bone of contention, and it was well worth a fight.

Striking out with his big right paw, the tame raccoon launched forth to secure the comb, whereupon Sintay struck at him with his disengaged paw, but refused to let go with the other. It was a ludicrous sight, and Wasula could not help laughing, especially when her pet succeeded in tearing away a part of the comb and the contents were generously daubed over their fur. But the fight soon became serious, and Wechah was getting the worst beating he had ever had when his mistress interfered. She struck at Sintay with her drawn bow and he dodged quickly behind the tree, still unwilling to leave it to the intruders, but at last he fled. It was the best thing for him to do!

Wechah stood before Wasula bleeding, his robe of fine fur sadly ruffled and plastered with honey and snow. He looked sorry for himself, yet proud of his discovery, and there was no time now to pity or rejoice. On they ran till, within hailing distance of the camp, the girl gave the wolf-call. The others were already very anxious. "She is coming!" they cried to one another, joyously, and two went forth to meet her, for her call meant a successful hunt.

Thus the maiden and her tame raccoon saved several families from starvation. The run of fish would last for days, and there was much honey in the tree, which they secured on the following day.

"It is my wish," said Wasula, "that you do not trap the 'coon again this season, for the sake of Wechah, who has saved us all. In gratitude to him, withdraw your deadfalls."

All agreed to this. Yet one spring morning when they were about to set out on the return journey he was not to be found, and no one had seen him. The huntress immediately took down her bow and quiver and searched for his track, which she followed into the woods. Her love for Wechah had never been fully realized by the people or perhaps even by herself. "If Sintay has met and taken revenge upon him, I shall not return without his scalp," she said to herself.

Over the still frozen lake to the nearest island lay Wechah's well-known track, and he was apparently hunting for company. It was the time of year when his people do so. He had run far and wide, meeting here and there a bachelor 'coon. The tracks told the story of how they merely dared one another and parted.

At last the trail lay over a slope overlooking a little cove, where there stood a large sugar-maple. The upper quarter of it had been torn off by lightning, leaving a very high stump. Wechah's tracks led directly to this tree, and the scratches on its bark plainly told who lived there. It was the home of Wechawee, the 'coon maid.

Wasula took her small hatchet from her belt and struck several quick blows. There was a scrambling inside, and in a moment Wechah poked his quaint striped face from the top. He looked very much abashed. Like a guilty dog he whined, but showed no desire to come down.

"Wechah, you frightened me! I thought you had been killed. I am glad now, my heart is good, that you have found your mate."

At this Wechah's new wife pushed her cunning head out beside that of her husband. Wasula stood looking at them both for a few minutes with mingled pleasure and sorrow, and ere she left she sang a maiden's serenade to the bridegroom—the founder of a new clan!

THE MUSTERING
OF THE HERDS

"Moo! Moo!" rang out the deep, air-rending call—the gathering call of the herds! Hinpoha, or Curly Hair, the young bison mother, threw back her head and listened nervously. She stood over her new-born baby in a hidden nook upon the Shaeyela River, that flows through the Land of Mystery.

No one was there to see, except two magpies which were loitering in the neighborhood, apparently waiting for the mother to go away that they might tease the helpless infant.

Tenderly she licked the moist hair of her dear one's coat, while the beautiful black-and-white bird with the long tail talked to his mate of mischief and plunder. Then the mother gently poked and pushed her little one, persuading her to get up and try her tiny, soft-soled feet. It was evident that she was not a common bison calf. Her color was not reddish brown, but a soft, creamy white, like that of a sheep—the color of royalty!

She toddled about unsteadily upon the thick mat of buffalo-grass. As she learned to walk, step by step, the young mother followed her with anxious eyes. Presently the little creature made a feeble attempt at running. She lifted up her woolly tail, elevated a pair of transparent, leaf-like ears, and skipped awkwardly around her mother, who never took her black, limpid eyes from her wonderful first-born.

"Moo! Moo!" Again Hinpoha heard the impatient gathering call. Hastily she pushed her baby with caressing nose into an old buffalo-wallow overhung with tall grass, making a little cosey nest. The drooping grass, like the robe of the Indian, concealed the little calf completely.

"You must stay here," she signed. "Do not open your eyes to any stranger. Do not move at all."

Hinpoha trotted northward, following the ravine in which she had hidden her calf. No sooner had she disappeared from sight than those old plunderers, magpie and his mate, swooped down from the lone willow-tree that overhung the spot. Both perched lightly upon the edge of the buffalo-wallow. They saw and heard nothing. They looked at each other in surprise. "Ka, ka, ka," they talked together, wondering what had become of the baby bison.

Up the long ascent Hinpoha ran, until she reached a point from which she could command the valley and the place where she had hidden away her treasure. Her watchful eyes ranged round the horizon and swept the surrounding country. There was not a wolf there, she thought. She could see the lone willow-tree that marked the spot. Beyond, the rough ridges and occasional buttes were studded with pines and cedars, while the white pillars and towers of the Bad Lands rose grandly in the distance.

As she went on to rejoin her herd upon the plains of the Shaeyela, she beheld upon the flats the bison women gathered in great, black masses, while on either side of them the buffalo men roamed in small groups or singly, like walking pine-trees. Shaeyela had never looked more lovely than on that morning in early spring—a warm, bluish haze brooding over it—the big, ungainly cotton-woods, their branches knotted and gnarled like the naked limbs of the old men, guarding the thin silver line of the river.

Hinpoha ran swiftly down the last descent, now and then pausing for a moment to announce her coming. Ordinarily she would have returned to her people quietly and unnoticed, but she was excited by the unexpected summons and moved to reply. As she entered the valley she saw other buffalo women returning from their spring nurseries in the gulches, giving their responses as they came. There was an undertone murmur throughout the great concourse. All seemed to be moving toward the edge of the belt of timber that clothed the river-banks. They pressed through a scattered growth of gray-green buffalo-berry bushes.

By the signs of the buffalo women and the sound of their lowings, Hinpoha knew that this was a funeral gathering. She hastened on with mingled curiosity and anxiety. Within a circle of the thorny buffalo-berry trees, under a shivering poplar, lay the lifeless form of Ptesan-wee, the white buffalo cow, the old queen of the Shaeyela herd.

Here all the dusky women of the plains had gathered to pay their last respects to their dead leader. Hinpoha pushed her way into the midst of the throng for a parting look. She joined in the wailing of the other bison women, and the noise of their mourning echoed like distant thunder from the opposite cliffs of the Shaeyela.

No bull buffalo was allowed to come near while the women hovered about their dead leader. These had to return to their nurseries at last, and then it was that the buffalo men approached in great numbers. The sound of their mourning was great! They tore up the sod with their hoofs as they wailed loudly for the dead.

The sun hovered over the western hills ere the gathering dispersed. The dead was left to the silent night to cover, and the lonely poplar sang a soft funeral song over her.

Hinpoha found her baby fast asleep when she reached her nursery upon Willow Creek. The little creature was fed, and played about her mother, grazing in the quiet valley, where none might see the cradle of their future queen.

At the next mid-day, Hinpoha saw many of the bison

people fleeing by her secret camp. She at once suspected the neighborhood of the Red hunters. "I shall go away, so that they will not find my teepee and my baby," she said to herself. Accordingly she came out and followed the trail of the fugitives in order to deceive the wild man, but at night she returned to her nursery.

Upon the Shaeyela River, below the camp of the buffalo people, the wild Red men were likewise encamped in great numbers. Spring was here at last, and nearly all of the snow had gone, even from the gulches and deep ravines.

A joyous hunting song pealed forth loudly from the council-lodge of the Two Kettle band. The great drum beat a prelude to the announcement heralded throughout the camp.

"Hear ye, hear ye, warriors! The game scout has come back with the news that the south fork of the Shaeyela is full of the buffalo people. It is the will of the council that the young men should now make the great spring hunt of the bison. Fill your quivers with good arrows. Try your bows. Heya, heya, ha-a-a-a!" Thus the herald circled the large encampment.

"Woo! woo!" came from the council-lodge—a soldier-call, for the young men to saddle up. At the same time, the familiar drum-beat was again heard. The old men, the council men, were now left alone to perform those ceremonies which were held to insure good hunting.

The long-stemmed pipe was reverently lifted from the

sacred ground which is its resting-place. The chief medicine-man, old Buffalo Ghost, took it in his sinewy hands,
with the mouth-piece foremost. He held it toward
heaven, then to the earth, and gave the "spirit talk."
Having ended, he lighted and passed it around the circle
from left to right. Again one struck the drum and sang in
a high minor key. All joined in the refrain, and two got
up and danced around the fire. This is done to call the
spirits of the bison, and charm them into a happy departure for the spirit land.

Meantime, the young warriors had mounted their
trained buffalo-ponies, and with a great crowd on foot
were moving up the valley of the Shaeyela. From every
divide they surveyed the country ahead, hoping to find
the buffalo in great numbers and to take them unawares.
The chief hunter ascended a hill in advance of the
others. "Woo!" he called, and waved his right hand with
the assurance of a successful hunt.

The warriors prepared for the charge just as they
would prepare for an attack upon the enemy. All prelimi-
nary orders were given. The men were lined out on
three sides, driving the herd toward the river. When the
signal was given, ponies and men sped forward with
loosened hair and flying lariat. The buffalo were
compelled to run toward the river, but some refused to
run, while many more broke through the attacking lines
and fled across the Shaeyela and into the woods. There
were some who stood their ground and formed an
outward-facing circle around the low little buffalo-berry-

hung grave. To this group many Red hunters came yelling and singing.

"Hanta, hanta yo!" the leader cautioned, vainly. The first man who ventured near the menacing circle was instantly tossed upon the horns of an immense bull. He lay motionless where he fell.

Now the angry bison were left alone for the time, while the hunters withdrew to a near-by hill for consultation. The signal of distress had been given, and soon the ridges were black with riders. The unfortunate hunter and his horse lay dead upon the plain!

"It is not the custom of the buffalo people to fight thus. They have been known to form a ring to defend themselves against wolves, but against man—never!" declared the game leader. "It is a sign of which we ought to discover the meaning."

"You have heard their lowing," remarked another. "It is their habit to mourn thus when they discover one of their number lying dead."

Suddenly the buffalo women started away in single file, the bulls following; and walking slowly, without molestation from any, they all disappeared in the direction taken by the fleeing herd. The hunters now eagerly advanced to the spot where lay dead the white bison cow, the queen of the buffalo people. The strange action of her followers was explained. Every warrior approached the place as if treading upon hallowed ground. They tied or hobbled their ponies at some distance, and all came with tobacco or arrows in their hands. They reverently addressed the dead cow and placed the tobacco gently around her for an offering. Thus strangely ended the first spring hunt of that year upon the Shaeyela, the ancient home of the buffalo people, where always the buffalo woman chief, the white cow, is seen—the most sacred and honored animal among the Sioux!

The grass of the Bad Lands region was now spread in fresh green, all beaded and porcupined with the early crocuses. The young queen was well grown for her age, and could run as well as her mother for a mile or two. Along Willow Creek she had been made to try her speed many times daily.

"Come," she signed to her, one bright May day, and they both set out for the forks of the Shaeyela, where once more the buffalo people were assembled by thousands. Many of the mothers had already taken their children back to the herd. As Hinpoha passed the lone bulls who are wont to wander away from the rest for undisturbed feeding, they all turned to gaze at her and her strange daughter. Each gave her sonorous greeting, and some even followed after at a distance in wonder and admiration.

When they reached a small group of buffalo women, there was much commotion. One of the other mothers came forward to challenge Hinpoha to a friendly contest, while the rest formed a ring around them, evidently admiring the little calf. The black eyes and hoofs setting off her creamy whiteness gave her a singularly picturesque appearance.

After the friendly tussle, the mother and daughter continued on their journey to the forks of the Shaeyela. As they passed more and more of their people, the "Moo" was given continuously, announcing the coming of the new queen of the tribe. When they arrived at the place of meeting, the excitement was great. Everywhere buffalo people were running toward them to greet them with the "Moo!" The little folks ran up full of curiosity, turned large eyes and ears on the stranger, and then fled away with uplifted tail. The big, shaggy-haired old men came, too, and regarded her gravely. Hinpoha was proud of her conspicuous position; yet it was a trying reception, for every kind female caller felt obliged to offer her a friendly trial of strength. At such times the little calf watched her mother with excited interest.

The day was warm, the air soft and summer-like. Whenever there is a great gathering of the bison, there are many contests and dances. So it was on this occasion. It was their festival time, and the rumble of their voices was heard by the other tribes of the prairie a great way off.

Again the herald's song pealed forth upon the sunshiny stillness of a May morning. Every ear was turned to catch the expected announcement of the wise men.

"Ye soldier hunters," was the summons, "come home

to the teyoteepee!" Many of the warriors, wrapped in their robes, walked slowly toward the council-lodge in the middle of the Indian encampment.

"Hear ye, men and warriors!" exclaimed the chief of the teyoteepee, when all were met together. "Our game scout has returned with the word that upon the forks of the Shaeyela the buffalo people are holding their summer gathering. Furthermore, he says that he saw a young buffalo chief woman—a white calf! In the morning all the hunters are commanded to make an attack upon the herd. If it be possible, we shall capture the little queen.

"Hear ye, hear ye! We shall dance the great buffalo-dance to-night! The Great Mystery is good to us. Few men are so favored as to see the queen of the buffalo people even once in a lifetime.

"Eyuha nahon po!" he continued, "hearken to the legend that is told by the old men. The buffalo chief woman is the noblest of all animals—the most beloved of her people. Where she is, there is the greatest gathering of her tribe—there is plenty for the Indian! They who see her shall be fortunate in hunting and in war. If she be captured, the people who take her need never go hungry. When the bison is scarce, the exhibition of her robe in the buffalo-dance will bring back many to the neighborhood!

"To-morrow we will make a great hunt. Be strong of heart, for her people will not flee, as is their wont, but will fight for her!"

"Ho, ho! hi, hi!" replied all the warriors.

The buffalo were now holding their summer feasts and dances upon the Shaeyela River—the tricky Shaeyela, who, like her sister, the Big Muddy, tears up her banks madly every spring freshet, thus changing her bed continually. The little hills define it abruptly, and the tributary creeks are indicated by a few dwarf pines and cedars, peeping forth like bears from the gulches. Upon the horizon the Bad Lands stand out in bold relief, their ruined pyramids and columns bespeaking the power of the Great Mystery.

Here at the forks the poplar-trees and buffalo-berry-bushes glistened in fresh foliage, and the deep-yellow flowers of the wild bull-currant exhaled their musky odor. There was a wide, green plain for the buffalo people to summer in, and many had come to see their baby queen, for the white bison was always found in the midst of the greatest gathering of her people. No chief buffalo woman was ever seen with a little band.

The morning was good; the sun wore a broad smile, and his children upon the Shaeyela River, both bison and wild Red men, were happy in their own fashion. The little fires were sportively burning outside of each teepee, where the morning meal had been prepared. It had been decreed by the council that the warriors should paint, after the custom of warfare, when they attacked the buffalo chief woman and her people upon the forks of the Shaeyela.

Upon the slope of a long ridge the hunters gathered. Their dusky faces and naked bodies were extravagantly

77

painted; their locks fantastically dressed; even the ponies were decorated. Upon the green plain below the bison were quietly grazing, and in the very centre of the host the little queen frisked about her mother. It was fully four arrow-flights distant from the outer edge of the throng, and sentinel bulls were posted still farther out, in precaution for her safety.

The Indians overlooking the immense herd had already pointed out the white calf in awe-struck whispers. To them she looked like an earth-visiting spirit in her mysterious whiteness. There were several thousand pairs of horns against their few hundred warriors, yet they knew that if they should succeed in capturing this treasure, the story would be told of them for generations to come. It was sufficient honor for the risk of a brave man's life.

"Hukahay! hukahay!" came the signal. Down the slope they sped to the attack with all the spirit and intrepidity of the gray wolf. "Woo! woo!" came from every throat in a hoarse shout. The earth under their ponies' feet fairly trembled.

The buffalo bull sentinels instantly gave the alarm and started back in the direction of the main body. A cloud of dust arose toward the sun as the mighty gathering was set in motion. Deadly arrows flew like winged things, and the beating of thousands of hoofs made a noise like thunder. Yet the buffalo people would not break the circle around the white calf, and for many minutes no Red man could penetrate it.

At last old Zuya, a warrior of note, came swiftly to the front upon his war-steed. He held high above his head a blazing torch, and the panic-stricken bison fled before him in every direction. Close behind him came Zuya's young son, Unspeshnee, with a long lariat coiled in his hand, and the two followed hard upon the fleeing buffalo people.

"Wa-wa-wa-wa!" came forth from hundreds of throats, like the rolling of many stones upon new ice. "Unspeshnee! Unspeshnee has lassoed the buffalo chief woman!"

Amid a great gathering of curious people stood the white calf, wailing continually, and a solemn rejoicing pervaded the camp of the Red hunters. Already the ceremonies were in progress to celebrate this event.

"It is the will of the Great Mystery," said they, "to recall the spirit of the white chief. We shall preserve her robe, the token of plenty and good-fortune! We shall never be hungry henceforth for the flesh of her nation. This robe shall be handed down from generation to generation, and wherever it is found there shall be abundance of meat for the Indian."

THE SKY WARRIOR

The all-night rain had ceased, and daylight appeared once more over the eastern buttes. Hooyah looked about her, anxiously scanning the gray dusk of morning for a glimpse of her mate, the while she spread her long pinions over three rollicking and mischievous youngsters as any eagle woman ever brooded. Her piercing gaze was directed oftenest toward the lone pine—his favorite sleeping-tree. Surely it was time for him to call her out on the usual morning hunt.

The Eagle's Nest butte was well known to the wild hunters of that region, since it could be seen from a great distance and by many approaches. Its overhanging sides were all but inaccessible, and from the level summit could be discerned all the landmarks of the Bad Lands in a circuit of seventy-five miles. The course of the Makezeta, the Smoking Earth River, lay unrolled like a map beneath that eyrie. Hither the bighorn, the grizzly, and others of the animal tribes had from time to time betaken themselves, some seeking a night's refuge and others a permanent dwelling-place. For many years, however, it had been well understood that this was the chosen home of Wambelee, the eagle, whom it is not well to molest.

Doubtless there have been tragedies enacted upon this imposing summit. There is even a tradition among the wild Red men that the supremacy upon old Eagle's Nest has cost many lives, and for this reason it is held to be a mysterious and hallowed place. Certainly the tribes of Wild Land had cause to desire and even to fight for its possession.

Suddenly there came to Hooyah's ears the whirring sound that announced the near approach of her master. In the wink of an eye he was at her side.

"Quick, quick! We must be off! I have found a doe with two small fawns. I could have taken one fawn, but we shall have more meat if you are there to take the other," he signalled to her.

Hooyah simply stepped aside and stretched herself thoroughly, as if to say, "Go, and I will follow."

Wambelee arose clumsily at the start, but as he gained in speed and balance he floated away in mid-air like a mystic cloud. Hooyah followed within hailing distance, and they kept the same relative positions until they reached Fishtail Gulch. It is well known to the Red hunters that such is the custom of the bear, coyote, eagle, raven and gray wolf, except when they travel in bands.

The rule is a good one, since the sought-for prey is less likely to take alarm when only one hunter is in sight, and then, in case of flight, the second pursuer, who is invisible, may have a better chance to make the capture, especially should the fleeing one double on his track. He is certain to be bewildered and disheartened by the sudden, unexpected reinforcement of the foe.

Wambelee swung up on one of the adjacent buttes to spy out possible danger, while his mate was balancing herself away up in the ether, just over the black-tail mother with her twin fawns. Suddenly he arose in a long spiral and ascended to the height of Hooyah, and there the two lotted their assault upon the innocents, at the same time viewing the secret movements of every other hunter.

It is the accepted usage of Wild Land that no one may wisely leave his tracks uncovered while he himself is on the trail of another, for many have been seized while enjoying the prize. Even the lordly eagle has been caught by the wolf, the wild-cat, or by the wild man while feasting, and in his gluttony has become an easy prey to the least of hunters. Therefore it behooved Wambelee to be watchful and very cautious.

"Ho, Opagela, koowah yay yo-o-o!" This was the call of Matoska, a famous hunter of the Sioux, at the door of his friend's lodge in the camp on the Smoking Earth River. "Come out, friend; it is almost day and my dream has been good. The game is plentiful; but you will need to be on your guard, for the tracks of the grizzly hereabout are as many as I have ever seen the Ojibway trails."

"Hun, hun, hay!" exclaimed the other, good-humoredly, as he pushed aside the triangular door-flap and appeared wrapped in his blanket. "It is always thus. When the hunting is poor, you will not be disturbed, but when you are in a region of much game, all other hunters are there as well! It is true that they are usually agreeable except two only—Mato, the grizzly, and man himself. These two are always looking for trouble!"

Opagela was likewise noted for his skill in hunting, and especially for the number of eagles that he had caught. This good-fortune had gained him many ponies, for eagles' feathers are always in demand. Few men so well understand the secrets of this bird. His friend was doubtless expert in wood-craft, but in this particular he could not claim to be the equal of Opagela.

"Come, let us hasten! We must be off before any other wild hunter can gain the advantage. We shall appear foolish to them if we are seen running about in full view," Matoska continued, as he adjusted the thongs of his moccasins.

Both men soon disappeared in the gray mists of the morning. They ran noiselessly side by side, scarcely uttering a word, up and along the bluffs of the Smoking Earth River. They could see the white vapor or breath of the bison hanging in the air at a distance, and black masses of the animals were visible here and there upon the plains. But they did not turn aside, for they were in search of other game. The Eagle's Nest butte loomed up to their right, its bare walls towering grandly above the surrounding country, and the big timber lay hidden below in the fog that still clung about the river.

"Ho!" Opagela exclaimed, presently, to his companion, in an undertone. "There is a hunter from above descending."

Both stood still in their tracks like petrified men. "Whir-r-r!" came like the sound of a coming shower.

"Ugh, it is he!" Opagela said again, in a whisper, and made a motion with his lips.

As the great bird, the giant hunter of the air, swooped down into the gulch, a doe fled forth from it and ran swiftly over the little divide. There was bawling and the sound of struggle just over the banks of the creek, where the eagle had disappeared.

"Run, friend, run! Let us see him use his knife upon the fawn," urged Matoska, and he started over the knoll at a good gait. The other followed as if reluctantly.

The little gulch was a natural enclosure formed by a sudden turn of the creek, and fenced with a thorny thicket of wild plum and buffalo-berry bushes. Here they saw Wambelee in the open, firmly fastened upon the back of a struggling fawn. Hooyah had missed her quarry, which took refuge in the plum grove.

"Shoot! shoot!" whispered Matoska, at the same time drawing forth an arrow.

"No, no; I recognize friends. This is the old pair who have dwelt for many years upon the Eagle's Nest butte." There was a serious expression upon the hunter's face as he spoke.

At this moment the eagle turned toward them. From his neck hung a single bear's claw, fastened by a leather thong.

"Yes, it is he. Long ago he saved my life, and we are friends. I shall tell you about it," Opagela said at last, and the two friends sat down side by side at the edge of the plum-bushes.

"Many winters ago," began Opagela, "I was shot through the knee in a battle with the Utes, a little west of the Black Hills. My friends carried me with them as far as the creek which is now called the Wounded Knee, and there we were overtaken by a Crow war-party. Our party had a running fight with them and were compelled to retreat in haste. I begged my friends to leave me on the trail, for I preferred to die fighting rather than from the effects of my wound. They did so, but before they reached me the Crow warriors withdrew.

"There I lay without food or water for four days. I was all skin and bones. My thoughts were already in the spirit land, and I seemed to see about me my relatives who had died.

"One morning my mind was clear, and once more I realized my surroundings. I had crawled into the shade of a little grove of plum-bushes. I gazed out upon the lofty buttes and the plains between where we had so often camped in happiness and plenty. It seemed hard to starve in the midst of such abundance.

"A few paces away I saw a doe with two fawns. They were fat and tempting, but I had no strength to shoot. Then I felt that I was doomed to die, and, indeed, believed that I was already half spirit and could talk with spirits. I held out my hand to the Great Mystery and said:

"Is this the end? Then, Great Father, I am resigned. Let none disturb me, for I would die in peace.

"At this moment the doe snorted and sprang directly over me. Alas! One of her little ones was caught before it could plunge into the thicket. It was seized by an immense eagle.

"The pretty little creature screamed and bawled like a baby, and my heart was with her in her death-pangs, although I was perishing for meat. I lay quite still and breathed softly. I slyly closed my eyes when the eagle seemed about to look in my direction. He appeared to be a very warlike, full-grown bird, with splendid plumage.

"He dressed his meat a few paces from me. I could smell the rich odor of the savory venison, and it made me desperate. I wanted to live now. But it was his game. I was a wounded, helpless, dying man—he a strong, warlike hunter. I could only beg a piece of his meat, but it was not the time for me to do so until he had eaten his fill.

"The zest with which he partook of his meal made me chew while he tore off pieces of the meat, and swallow whenever he swallowed a savory morsel. At last I could not endure it any longer.

"'Ho, kola!' I said, feebly.

"The sky warrior lifted his noble head with the mien of a great chief. At first he did not discover where the voice came from, but, nevertheless, he made a show of indignation and surprise.

"Again I said, almost in a whisper, 'Ho, kola, it is time you should cheer a dying warrior's heart.'

"He saw me. 'Hush-h-h!' he sighed, and released his great talons from the body of the fawn.

"My mind was clear now, and the sight of meat seemed to give me strength. I took my long knife in one hand and my war-club in the other, and I rose and hopped towards him. He tried to fly, but could not. This is his greatest weakness—that when he kills big game he surfeits himself and is sometimes unable to fly for half a day or longer. As the eagle is not a good walker, he could not get away from me. All his dignity disappeared. Help-less as a woman, he lay before me with outstretched wings.

"I had no wish to harm him who had preserved my life. I lassoed him with my lariat and fastened him to a plum-tree while I ate of the meat. It was tender and luscious, and my strength returned to me even as I ate.

"I could not walk, so Wambelee and I camped together, for I did not care to be alone. Little by little we became friends. On the second day his wife came in search of him. When she found him a captive she scolded violently, perhaps him alone, perhaps me, or both of us.

"The next time she came prepared to make war upon me in order to release her husband. She appeared high up, floating among the clouds; then suddenly gave a scream, woman-like, and shot down with all the fierceness of a warrior, coming directly toward me.

"I was getting strong now, and I shook my bow over my head at her. Then she swung upward within a few bows' length, so that I could feel the wind of her attack.

"After she had done this several times, she perched upon a near-by butte and watched. She did everything in her power to make her captive husband's heart strong. Now and then she would sail slowly over our heads, coaxing, scolding, and apparently having a loving, conjugal talk with him.

"At last I sat beside her mate and gave him some meat, which he took from my hand. She saw this feast of two warrior-friends, and came within a few paces of us. I threw her a piece of the venison, which she took, and ate of it.

"Our meat was now gone, and we moved nearer to the stream. I awoke early in the morning. Wambelee was uneasy, and stared continually into the gray dusk. I looked in the same direction, and I saw four black-tail deer approaching the water to drink. I had tied one end of Wambelee's lariat to a young sapling, and let him sit by me, concealed under the bushes. He had a long lariat. When the deer were almost upon us, I took my sharpest arrow and shot the buck deer. At the same time Wambelee secured a fawn. Now we were rich, for we had all the meat we wanted!

"When we first moved our camp, the eagle woman did not like it, because she did not understand. But again she came every day and got rations for herself and her eaglets on the nest. It was a day's run for a warrior from the Eagle's Nest butte to the place where we were upon the Wounded Knee.

"I was now strong and able to walk a short distance. Wambelee and Hooyah had become my good friends. They feared me no longer. One day I said to him:

"'My friend, you have saved my life. I am strong again, and I shall return to my people. You also must go back to your children. I have three in my lodge, and you should have as many. See, I will give you a necklace—a brave's necklace—before you go.'

"I took one claw from my necklace of bears' claws, and tied it about his neck with a leather thong. I also cut a little figure of a man out of a deer's hoof, and tied it to the eagle woman's neck.

"'You have been a faithful and brave wife to my friend Wambelee,' I said to her. 'You shall have this for a token from his friend.'

"Then I released Wambelee. He stepped aside, but showed no sign of going. The eagle woman simply busied herself with cutting out a piece of venison to take to her hungry children.

"'I see that you are true friends. I will take two feathers from each of you,' I said.

"I took two feathers from each and stuck them in my head. The eagle woman rose with the meat, but Wambelee still stood by me. I said, 'Go, friend, it is time,' and reluctantly he rose and followed her.

"When they had left me it was lonely, and I could not stay. I took my lariat and my weapons and walked slowly up the creek, which was then called Blacktail Creek. From that day it has been known as the Wounded Knee.

"Before sunset, Wambelee came back to see where I was. I was compelled to travel very slowly, and they watched and followed me from day to day until I reached home. There I was as one returned from the dead.

"Nor is this all. In my journeyings these two have many times come near me. I have a signal-call for them, and they have one for me. They have been my guide to game, and I have shared my game with them."

Opagela thus ended his story. Matoska had listened with an attentive ear and a respect that bordered upon reverence.

"It is well, friend," he said, finally, with marked significance.

The two old eagles had busied themselves meanwhile with their game, eating a part and preparing part to take to their children. They now showed signs of age. Their coats were of a brownish color, and their tail-feathers creamy white.

Opagela filled his pipe and held it toward them in

token of his good wishes. Then he offered it to his companion.

"We shall smoke," he said, "to their long life and success in hunting." Matoska silently nodded assent.

"And how is it, friend, that you kill so many eagles?" he asked, at last.

"I have never killed one," said Opagela. "I have caught many, but without harm to them. I take several of the tail-feathers and let them go. Because I have always many eagle feathers, the warriors think that I kill them.

"Sinkpay both captures and kills them," he continued. "He makes a fish out of a water-soaked log. He whittles it to the shape of a fish, puts a weight on it, and ties it to a long rope which he holds from the shore of a certain lake. You know the eagle is a good fisherman, and when he sees from a great height the make-believe fish of Sinkpay, he drops down very swiftly and buries his claws deeply in the spongy wood. Then Sinkpay pulls this wooden fish to shore with the eagle clinging to it, because he cannot pull out his long, crooked talons. Always his greed is his destruction," concluded the hunter.

"And how do you catch yours?" quoth Matoska.

"Upon a hill frequented by eagles, I dig a hole and lie in it, covered with brush, and holding up a freshly killed rabbit. The eagle sees the rabbit a great way off, and he will immediately shoot down and seize it. I catch him by the leg and pull him down into the hole. There I tie his feet and pull out several of his tail-feathers.

"You will never catch an eagle twice with the same

trick. My old friends know all about it, and delight to play with me by tearing the skin of the bait while hovering out of reach."

"And how do you recognize those two old eagles?" again asked Matoska.

"I know them as well as you know one man from another. You cannot doubt me, for you see their necklaces.

"I have kept this matter sacred and secret for many years. It is not well to talk of the favors of the Great Mystery. But you have seen my friend the sky warrior and his wife, therefore I told it to you. You will not speak of it?" the old hunter asked his friend, who nodded gravely. The two old eagles, laden with their prey, flew heavily away in the direction of the Eagle's Nest.

A FOUNDER OF TEN TOWNS

U pon a grassy plateau, overlooking the flats of
the Owl River, was spread out Pezpeza's
town. The borders of the table-land were
defined by the river's bed, and it was sufficiently high for
the little inhabitants to command the valley both up and
down for a considerable distance. Shungela Pahah, or
Fox Ridge, stretched upward on the horizon, and the
rough country back of it formed many ravines and
gulches for the solitary habitations of wolves and foxes.

No prettier site could be imagined for a town of the
prairie-dog people, among whom there is no more enterprising frontiersman than Pezpeza. Although it was situ-
ated in plain view of one of the large summer camps of
the wild Sioux, the little people had been left unmolested.
The wild men lived then in the midst of the greatest
game region of the Dakotas, and, besides, they had

always looked upon the little mound-builders as having once been real people like themselves.

All over the plateau, which was semicircular in form, were scattered hundreds of mounds, and on that particular morning, when the early Sioux hunter rode by upon his favorite pony, every house was alive with the inhabitants. Upon the mounds of the old deserted houses stood the faithful and good neighbor, Pezpeza ta ayanpahalah, Pezpeza's herald, the owl; for if any house is left vacant, he immediately occupies it. Here and there, upon a sun-baked mound, lay coiled the other neighbor, Sintay-hadah, the rattlesnake.

The herald had announced the coming of the wild Red man upon his hunting pony; therefore every prairie-dog had repaired to the top of the mound beside his dwelling. Some stood upon their hind-legs, that they might better see for themselves the approaching danger, and from this place of safety they all shrilly scolded the intruders; while the little herald, who had done his duty and once more fulfilled his unspoken contract with his hosts to be their scout and crier, perched calmly upon a chosen mound and made his observations.

In the middle of the town, upon a large mound, there stood an unusually large dog. When the warning was given, he had slowly dragged himself outside. His short, thick fur was much yellower than that of the others, a sign of advancing age; and while the citizens were noisy in their protests, he alone was silent. It was Pezpeza, the founder of this town and of many another, the experienced traveller. His old friend, the faithful herald, who had just given warning, perched not far away. These two had journeyed together and shared each other's hardships, but Pezpeza was the prime mover in it all, and there was none wiser than he among his people.

Pezpeza's biographer and interpreter tells thus of his wonderful frontier life and adventures.

Pezpeza was one of many children of an old couple who lived upon the Missouri River bottoms. He had learned while yet small that the little prairie-owl was their very good neighbor and friend. He had repaired and occupied one of their abandoned houses. It was generally understood by the little mound-builders that this quiet, unassuming bird notifies them of approaching danger; and, having no bad habits, the prairie-dogs had tacitly accepted them as desirable and useful townsfolk. The owl, for his part, finds a more convenient home and better food in the towns than he could possibly find elsewhere, for there are plants peculiar to the situation which attract certain insects, mice, and birds, and these in turn furnish food for the owls.

Their common neighbor, the rattlesnake, lay at times under a strong suspicion of treachery, and was not liked any too well by the other two. However, the canny and cold-hearted snake had proved his usefulness beyond any doubt, and was accepted under strict and well-understood conditions. He was like the negro in the South—he was permitted to dwell in the same town, but he must not associate with the other two upon equal terms. It is clear that the dog and the owl together could whip and terrorize the snake and force him to leave the premises at any time if they felt so disposed, but there is a sufficient reason for allowing him to remain. The wolf, coyote, fox, swift, and badger, all enemies of the little mound-builders, will not linger long in the neighborhood of rattlesnakes, and this is equally true of the Red hunter. The coyote and badger could easily lie flat behind the mound and spring upon the prairie-dog when he comes out of his hole. The Sioux boy could do the same with his horse-hair noose. But these wild hunters, with full knowledge of the deadly rattlesnake, dare not expose themselves in such a fashion. The snake, on his side, gets his food much easier there than anywhere else, since all kinds of small birds come there for seeds. Further, his greatest enemies are certain large birds which do not fear his poison, but swoop down, seize him, and eat him in mid-air. From this danger he is safer in a dog-town than elsewhere, owing to the multitude of holes, which are ingeniously dug upward and off at one side from the main burrow, and are much better than the snake can provide for himself.

Pezpeza was like all the young people of his tribe. He loved play, but never played with the snake young people —on the contrary, he would stand at a safe distance and upbraid them until they retired from his premises. It was not so with the children of the little herald, the owl. In fact, he had played with them ever since he could remember, and the attachment between them became permanent. Wherever Pezpeza goes, the little owl always comes and sits near-by upon some convenient mound. If any hawk is in sight, and if he should see it first, he would at once give the warning and Pezpeza would run for his house.

Every day some prairie-dog left the town in quest of a new home. The chief reason for this is over-population —hence, scarcity of food; for the ground does not yield a sufficient quantity for so many.

One morning, as he was coming out of their house, Pezpeza found his father lying dead within the entrance. At first he would not go by, but at last he left the house, as did the rest of the family. None returned to their old home. The mother and children built a new house on the edge of the town, dangerously near a creek, and the old homestead was after that owned by a large rattlesnake family who had always loafed about the place. The new home was a good one, and the new ground yielded an abundant crop, but they were harassed by the wolves and wild-cats, because they were near the creek and within easy approach.

Pezpeza was out feeding one morning with a brother when all at once the owl gave the warning. They both ran for the house, and Pezpeza got in safe, but his brother was carried off by a wolf.

When he came out again, the place was not like what it used to be to him. He had a desire to go somewhere else, and off he started without telling any one. He followed an old buffalo-trail which lay over the plain and up the Owl River.

The river wound about among the hills and between deeply cut banks, forming wide bottom-lands, well timbered with cottonwoods. It was a warm day of blue haze in the early spring, and Pezpeza ran along in excellent spirits. Suddenly a warning screech came from behind, and he lay flat, immovable, upon the path. Ah, it is his friend the young herald, the owl playmate! The owl had seen his young friend run away over the prairie, so he flew to join him, giving no thought to his people or his own affairs.

The herald flew ahead and perched upon a convenient mound until his friend came up; then he went ahead again. Thus the two travelled over the plain until they came to a point where many buffalo skulls lay scattered over the ground. Here, some years before, the Red men had annihilated a herd of buffalo in a great hunt.

As usual, the herald flew ahead and took up his position upon a buffalo skull which lay nose downward. The skull was now bleached white, but the black horns were still attached to it. The herald sat between these horns.

Meanwhile Pezpeza was coming along the buffalo-path at a fairly good speed. Again he heard the danger-call and ran for the nearest skull to hide. He was glad to find that the thin bones of the nose were gone, so that he could easily enter it. He was not any too quick in finding a refuge, for a large eagle swooped down with a rush and sat by the skull. Pezpeza had crouched in the inner cavity, and when he was discovered he made a great show of indignation and fight. But the eagle, having made a careful study of the position of his intended victim, finally flew away, and in due time Pezpeza proceeded on his journey.

He did not go far, but when he had found a level, grassy plateau, commanding all the approaches, he began without delay to dig a home for himself, for he is not safe a moment without a home. The herald sat a little way off upon a stray bowlder, and occasionally he would fly out for a short distance and then return.

The sun hovered over Fox Ridge, and long columns of shadow were cast by the hills. Pezpeza, weary with his journey and the work of digging a home at least deep enough for a night's occupancy, had laid himself away in it to sleep. The herald, as usual, constituted himself a night-watch, and perched upon the newly made mound. There he sat with his head sunk deep in his soft feathers.

No sooner had the sun set in the west than the full moon appeared in the east, but the owl still sat motionless. He did not move even when a gray wolf came trotting along the buffalo-trail. When he came opposite the mound he stopped and held his muzzle low. At last he cautiously advanced, and when he was dangerously near the owl flew away and the wolf rushed upon the mound, and stood for a while peering into the hole.

It was now the herald's turn to annoy. It is true he cannot do anything more than bluff, but he is skilled in that. Especially at night, his gleaming eyes and the snapping of his bill, together with his pretentious swoop, make even the gray wolf nervous, and it was not long before he had decided to go farther.

The next morning the enterprising town-builder earnestly went about completing his home, although one could see only the little mound and the cup-shaped entrance—all else was deep underground. Every day there were arrivals, singly or in couples, and now and then a whole family. Nearly all brought their heralds with them, and these, likewise, came singly or in pairs. Immediately, each couple would go to work to prepare a dwelling for themselves, for they are not safe without them, and, besides, they seem to believe in independent homes. Thus in one moon the town became a respectably large one.

Shunkmanitoo, the wolf, had many a time trotted over the plateau and seen either a lone buffalo bull grazing or lying down chewing his cud, or an antelope standing cautiously in the middle that he might better see the approach of any danger. Now, after a few days' absence, he found a flourishing village, and one by no means devoid of interest and attraction.

Every bright day the little people played "catch-the-laugh." It is so called by the Red people. When all were outside their houses, one would jump into the air and make a peculiar sound, half squeak and half growl. The nearest one would take it up, and so on throughout the village. All would rise on their hind-feet and bob up and down, at the same time giving the peculiar cry. This performance they repeat whenever they are happy.

Pezpeza's town was now quite populous. But he was not the mayor; he did not get any credit for the founding of the town; at least as far as the Red people could observe. Their life and government seemed to be highly democratic. Usually the concentration of population produced a certain weed which provided abundance of food for them. But under some conditions it will not grow; and in that case, as soon as the native buffalo-grass is eaten up the town is threatened with a famine, and the inhabitants are compelled to seek food at a distance from their houses. This is quite opposed to the habit and safety of the helpless little people. Finally the only alternative will be the desertion of the town.

Thus it happened that Pezpeza, when the buffalo-grass was all gone about his place, began to realize the necessity of finding a new home. The ground was not adapted to the crop that generally grew in a prairie-dog town. One morning he was compelled to go beyond the limits of the village to get his breakfast, and all at once the thought of going off in search of a good town-site seized him strongly. He consulted no one, not even his best friend, the owl. He simply ran away up the river.

The buffalo-trails were many and well beaten. He followed one of them—he knew not whither. The herald soon discovered his departure and again followed his friend. Pezpeza was glad to see him fly past and take the lead, as usual.

The trail now led them to the brow of the table-land. Below them, along the river-bottoms, great herds of buffalo grazed among the shady cottonwood groves, and the path led down the slope. It was safer for the little town-maker to get among the big, burly bison, for the wolf does not go among them at such times. It is usually just beyond the herd that he peeps from behind the hills, watching for a chance to attack an isolated cow.

The buffalo did not pay any attention to the little fellow running on the trail and almost under their feet. They even allowed the herald to perch upon an old bull's back in order to keep within sight of his friend. Through the great herd the two proceeded. It was hot, and the grass was all eaten off close to the ground. There was no food for the little traveller.

He had descried a fair plateau on the opposite side of the Owl River as he came down the hill, and his mind was fixed upon this land. He was heading for the river, but found himself much hampered by the increasing number of the buffalo.

At the edge of the bank which marked the old bed of the stream Pezpeza came to a stand-still. Here the trail entered the woods and the bison followed it in single file. As they skirted the bank they passed so near him that their broad backs were almost within his reach, and some of them stopped for a moment to rub themselves against its steep sides. Finally there came an old bull with horns worn almost to the skull. He stopped just below Pezpeza and dug his stumpy horn into the earth wall, and

Pezpeza sprang gently upon his back and flattened himself out as thin as he could.

The bull did not suspect that anything unusual had happened. He supposed that what he felt was merely a lump of dirt that he had loosened with his horns, and off he walked quite unconcernedly on the trail towards the river. Many of his people were already crossing, and he followed them. The herald was perched upon the back of another bull, and so the pair crossed the Owl River.

There was a broad meadow-land through which the trail led up on the other side until it lost itself in a sage-bush plain. Here the bison scattered to graze, and many followed the ravines for better grass. Pezpeza let himself slide from the bull's back, who gave a jump and a snort, but it was too late to enter a protest.

The little town-builder now began his work as faithfully as before, and soon founded another large town. But again the misfortunes of life compelled him and his friend to leave the place. Thus they travelled up the river, now upon one side and now the other, and never more than a day's journey. More than once Pezpeza found a mate, and he raised many a family; but, like a true pioneer, he could never remain long in an old and over-crowded town.

His tenth and last home was the beautiful table-land at the junction of Owl River with Lost Creek. As has been described in the beginning, it was a semicircular plain of large extent and commanded a striking view. At the very head of the embankment, which sloped abruptly down to the river level, there stood a number of large grassy mounds, and among them were several peculiar structures composed of poles placed upright in the ground with others arranged horizontally so as to form a sort of shelter.

The town-maker gave no serious thought to these things. The grass upon the plateau was excellent, and he set to work at once, selecting a site for his home near the centre of the plain, for greater safety. Every day new-comers came, and it was a source of satisfaction to him that his selection was such as every prairie-dog could not but approve. In a few days the town was fairly started.

There arrived one day a family who took up their claim close by Pezpeza's place. In this family there was a pretty maid, according to Pezpeza's notion and fancy. There was no reason why he should not think so, for he was now a widower, a wolf having carried off his faithful mate of several years' standing. It was soon noticed by the other little people that the pretty maid with garments the color of the buffalo-grass in autumn had gone to live with Pezpeza.

Pezpeza's town was now a place of respectable size, well known in all that region. The coyote and gray wolf knew it well; the Red man also, for, as I said in the beginning, their favorite summer camp was not far away, and there they were wont to dance the "sun dance" at every midsummer.

At times the Red men were seen to come and roam, singing, around the large mounds and the curious scaffolds, and before they went away they would place one of their number upon a new scaffold or heap another mound. Still the little people gave no thought to these strange actions.

Many, many of their tribe came from all directions, until Pezpeza's town might almost be called a city. Many children were born there. The plateau was alive with the little mound-builders, who constantly built their homes farther and farther out, till at last some had built right under the Red men's scaffolds and hard by the large mounds, which were the graves of their dead.

Pezpeza's ground did not yield its usual crop any more. His children were all grown and had homes of their own. For some reason he did not care to go far away, so the old folks simply moved out to the edge of the town.

Pezpeza was now old and very large and fat. Never had he known for so long a time a happy home as in the town upon the "scaffold plain," as the place was called by the Red people. When they came to visit the graves of their dead they had never troubled the little mound-builders, therefore the old founder of many towns did not think of danger when he built very near to one of the scaffolds, and there were others who did the same.

On a bright autumn morning, early risers among the little people saw one of the Red men standing under a newly built scaffold and wailing loudly. He was naked and painted black. Many of the young people of the town barked at him as he stood there in their midst, and some of the young heralds, disturbed by the noise of his wailing, flew about and alighted upon the scaffolds. When he ceased mourning, he turned about and talked long at the little people and then went away.

The angry mourner reported at the great camp that the prairie-dogs and their owls were desecrating the graves, and it was time that they should be driven away. A council was held, and the next day the Red men came with their dogs and killed many. Their arrows pinned many of them to the ground before they could dodge into their holes. Then they scattered all over the town and remained there, so that none dared to come out. The owls were shot or driven away, and the Red men killed every rattlesnake that they found. It was an awful time! During the night many of the little people went away, deserting their homes.

The next day the same thing happened again, and the Red men even stopped up the entrances to many of the houses with round stones. Again in the night many of the little mound-builders left the town.

On the third day they came and set fire to the plain. After that, in the night, all the remaining population abandoned the town, except only Pezpeza. All this time the founder of the ten towns had remained in-doors. He was old and reluctant to move. At last he emerged with his mate. An awful sight met their eyes. On the blackened plain not one of the great population could be seen. Not one of their many children and grandchildren was there to greet them or to play at "catch-the-laugh"!

As soon as they dared the two old people sought food under the scaffolds, where the grass was not burned. Two Red men arose from behind a grave and let their arrows fly. Alas! the aged leader of the mound-builders was pinned to the ground. His mate barely escaped a similar fate, for the other missed.

The herald saw everything that had happened. He took up his watch from the centre of the ruined town. The sun went down, moonlight flooded the prairie, and he heard the evening call of the coyotes upon Fox Ridge. At last he saw something moving—it was the widowed mate of his friend, running along the trail from the desolate town. He gave one last look about him, then he silently rose and followed her.

THE GRAY CHIEFTAIN

O
n the westernmost verge of Cedar Butte
stood Haykinshkah and his mate. They
looked steadily toward the setting sun, over a
landscape which up to that time had scarcely been
viewed by man—the inner circle of the Bad Lands.

Cedar Butte guards the southernmost entrance to
that wonderland, standing fully a thousand feet above the
surrounding country, and nearly half a mile long by a
quarter of a mile wide. The summit is a level, grassy
plain, its edges heavily fringed with venerable cedars. To
attempt the ascent of this butte is like trying to scale the
walls of Babylon, for its sides are high and all but inaccessible. Near the top there are hanging lands or terraces
and innumerable precipitous points, with here and there
deep chimneys or abysses in the solid rock. There are
many hidden recesses and more than one secret entrance
to this ancient castle of the gray chieftain and his ances-

tors, but to assail it successfully requires more than common skill and spirit.

Many a coyote had gone up as high as the second leaping-bridge and there abandoned the attempt. Old grizzly had once or twice begun the ascent with doubt and misgiving, but soon discovered his mistake, and made clumsy haste to descend before he should tumble into an abyss from which no one ever returns. Only Igmutanka, the mountain-lion, had achieved the summit, and at every ascent he had been well repaid; yet even he seldom chose to risk such a climb, when there were many fine hunting-grounds in safer neighborhoods.

So it was that Cedar Butte had been the peaceful home of the big spoonhorns for untold ages. To be sure, some of the younger and more adventurous members of the clan would depart from time to time to found a new family, but the wiser and more conservative were content to remain in their stronghold. There stood the two patri-archs, looking down complacently upon the herds of buffalo, antelope, and elk that peopled the lower plains. While the sun hovered over the western hills, a coyote upon a near-by eminence gave his accustomed call to his mate. This served as a signal to all the wild hunters of the plains to set up their inharmonious evening serenade, to which the herbivorous kindred paid but little attention. The phlegmatic spoonhorn pair listened to it all with a fine air of indifference, like that of one who sits upon his own balcony, superior to the passing noises of the street.

It was a charming moonlight night upon the cedar-fringed plain, and there the old chief presently joined the others in feast and play. His mate sought out a secret resting-place. She followed the next gulch, which was a perfect labyrinth of caves and pockets, and after leaping two chasms she reached her favorite spot. Here the gulch made a square turn, affording a fine view of the country through a window-like opening. Above and below this were perpendicular walls, and at the bottom a small cavity, left by the root of a pine which had long since fallen and crumbled into dust. To this led a narrow terrace—so narrow that man or beast would stop and hesitate long before venturing upon it. The place was her own by right of daring and discovery, and the mother's instinct had brought her here to-night, for the pangs of deadly sickness were upon her.

In a little while relief came, and the ewe stood over a new-born lamb, licking tenderly the damp, silky hair, and trimming the little hoofs of their cartilaginous points. The world was quiet now, and those whose business it is to hunt or feed at night must do so in silence, for such is the law of the plains. The wearied mother slept in peace.

The sun was well above the butte when she awoke, although it was cool and shadowy still in her concealed abode. She gave suck to the lamb and caressed it for some time before she reluctantly prepared its cradle, according to the custom of her people. She made a little pocket in the side of the cave and gently put her baby in. Then she covered him all up, save the nose and eyes, with dry soil. She put her nose to his little sensitive ear and breathed into it warm love and caution, and he felt and understood that he must keep his eyes closed and breathe gently, lest bear or wolf or man should spy him out when they had found her trail. Again she put her warm, loving nose to his eyes, then patted a little more earth on his body and smoothed it off. The tachinchana closed his eyes in obedience, and she left him for the plain above in search of food and sunlight.

At a little before dawn, two wild hunters left their camp and set out for Cedar Butte. Their movements were marked by unusual care and secrecy. Presently they hid their ponies in a deep ravine and groped their way up through the difficult Bad Lands, now and then pausing to listen. The two were close friends and rival hunters of their tribe.

"I think, friend, you have mistaken the haunts of the spoonhorn," remarked Wacootay, as the pair came out upon one of the lower terraces. He said this rather to test his friend, for it was their habit thus to criticise and question each other's judgment, in order to extract from each other fresh observations. What the one did not know about the habits of the animals they hunted in common the other could usually supply.

"This is his home—I know it," replied Grayfoot. "And in this thing the animals are much like ourselves. They will not leave an old haunt unless forced to do so either by lack of food or overwhelming danger."

They had already passed on to the next terrace and leaped a deep chasm to gain the opposite side of the butte, when Grayfoot suddenly whispered, "In ahjin!" (Stop!). Both men listened attentively. "Tap, tap, tap," an almost metallic sound came to them from around the perpendicular wall of rock.

"He is chipping his horns!" exclaimed the hunter, overjoyed to surprise the chieftain at this his secret occupation. "Poor beast, they are now too long for him, so that he cannot reach the short grass to feed. Some of them die starving, when they have not the strength to do the hard bucking against the rock to shorten their horns. He chooses this time, when he thinks no one will hear him, and he even leaves his own clan when it is necessary for him to do this. Come, let us crawl up on him unawares."

They proceeded cautiously and with cat-like steps around the next projection, and stood upon a narrow strip of slanting terrace. At short intervals the pounding noise continued, but strain their eyes as they might they could see nothing. Yet they knew that a few paces from them, in the darkness, the old ram was painfully driving his horns against the solid rock. Finally they lay flat upon the ground under a dead cedar, the color of whose trunk and that of the scanty soil somewhat resembled their clothing, and on their heads they had stuck some bunches of sage-bush, to conceal them from the eyes of the spoonhorn.

With the first gray of the approaching dawn the two

hunters looked eagerly about them. There stood, in all his majesty, heightened by the wild grandeur of his surroundings, the gray chieftain of the Cedar Butte! He had no thought of being observed at that hour. Entirely unsuspicious of danger, he stood alone upon a pedestal-like terrace, from which vantage-point it was his wont to survey the surrounding country every morning. If the secret must be told, he had done so for years, ever since he became the head chief of the Cedar Butte clan.

It is the custom of their tribe that when a ram attains the age of five years he is entitled to a clan of his own, and thereafter must defend his right and supremacy against all comers. His experience and knowledge are the guide of his clan. In view of all this, the gray chieftain had been very thorough in his observations. There was not an object anywhere near the shape of bear, wolf, or man for miles around his kingdom that was not noted, as well as the relative positions of rocks and conspicuous trees.

The best time for Haykinshkah to make his daily observations is at sunrise and sunset, when the air is usually clear and objects appear distinct. Between these times the clan feed and settle down to chew their cud and sleep, yet some are always on the alert to catch a passing stranger within their field of observation. But the old chief spoonhorn pays very little attention. His duty is done. He may be nestled in a gulch just big enough to hold him, either sound asleep or leisurely chewing his cud. The younger members of the clan take their position upon the upper terraces and under the shade of projecting rocks, after a whole night's feasting and play upon the plain.

As spoonhorn stood motionless, looking away off toward the distant hills, the plain below appeared from this elevated point very smooth and sheetlike, and every moving object a mere speck. His form and color were not very different from the dirty gray rocks and clay of the butte.

Wacootay broke the silence. "I know of no animal that stands so long without movement, unless it is the turtle. I think he is the largest ram I have ever seen."

"I am sure he did not chip where he stands now," remarked Grayfoot. "This chipping-place is a monastery to the priests of the spoonhorn tribe. It is their medicine-lodge. I have more than once approached the spot, but could never find the secret entrance."

"Shall I shoot him now?" whispered his partner in the chase.

"No, do not do it. He is a real chief. He looks mysterious and noble. Let us know him better. Besides, if we kill him now we shall never see him again. Look! he will fall to that deep gulch ten trees' length below, where no one can get at him."

As Grayfoot spoke the animal shifted his position, facing them squarely. The two men closed their eyes and wrinkled their motionless faces into the semblance of two lifeless mummies. The old sage of the mountains was apparently deceived, but after a few moments he got down from his lofty position and disappeared around a point of rock.

"I never care to shoot an animal while he is giving me a chance to know his ways," explained Grayfoot. "We have plenty of buffalo meat. We are not hungry. All we want is spoons. We can get one or two sheep by-and-by, if we have more wit than they."

To this speech Wacootay agreed, for his curiosity was now fully aroused by Grayfoot's view, although he had never thought of it in just that way before. It had always been the desire for meat which had chiefly moved him in the matter of the hunt.

Having readjusted their sage wigs, the hunters made the circuit of the abyss that divided them from the ram, and as they looked for his trail they noticed the tracks of a large ewe leading down toward the inaccessible gulches.

"Ah, she has some secret down there! She never leaves her clan like this unless it is to steal away on a personal affair of her own."

So saying, Grayfoot with his fellow tracked the ewe's footprint along the verge of a deep gulf with much trouble and patience. The hunter's curiosity and a strong desire to know her secret impelled the former to lead the way.

"What will be our profit, if one slips and goes down into the gulch, never to be seen again?" remarked Wacootay, as they approached a leaping-place. The chasm below was of a great depth and dark. "It is not wise for us to follow farther; this ewe has no horns that can be made into spoons."

"Come, friend; it is when one is doubting that mishaps are apt to occur," urged his companion.

"Koda, heyu yo!" exclaimed Wacootay, the next moment, in distress.

"Hehehe, koda! Hold fast!" cried the other.

Wacootay's moccasined foot had slipped on the narrow trail, and in the twinkling of an eye he had almost gone down a precipice of a hundred feet; but with a desperate launch forward he caught the bough of an overhanging cedar and swung by his hands over the abyss.

Quickly Grayfoot pulled both their bows from the quivers. He first tied himself to the trunk of the cedar with his packing-strap, which always hung from his belt. Then he held both the bows toward his friend, who, not without difficulty, changed his hold from the cedar bough to the bows. After a short but determined effort, the two men stood side by side once more upon the narrow foothold of the terrace. Without a word they followed the ewe's track to the cave.

Here she had lain last night. Both men began to search for other marks, but they found not so much as a sign of scratching anywhere. They examined the ground closely without any success. All at once a faint "Ba-a-a!" came from almost under their feet. They saw a puff of smokelike dust as the little creature called for its mother.

It had felt the footsteps of the hunters and mistaken them for those of its own folk.

Wacootay hastily dug into the place with his hands and found the soil loose. Soon he uncovered a little lamb. "Ba-a-a!" it cried again, and quick as a flash the ewe appeared, stamping the ground in wrath.

Wacootay seized an arrow and fitted it to the string, but his companion checked him.

"No, no, my friend! It is not the skin or meat that we are looking for. We want horn for ladles and spoons. The mother is right. We must let her babe alone."

The wild hunters silently retreated, and the ewe ran swiftly to the spot and took her lamb away.

"So it is," said Grayfoot, after a long silence, "all the tribes of earth have some common feeling. I believe they are people as much as we are. The Great Mystery has made them what they are. Although they do not speak our tongue, we often seem to understand their thought. It is not right to take the life of any of them unless necessity compels us to do so.

"You know," he continued, "the ewe conceals her lamb in this way until she has trained it to escape from its enemies by leaping up or down from terrace to terrace. I have seen her teaching the yearlings and two-year-olds to dive down the face of a cliff which was fully twice the height of a man. They strike on the head and the two fore-feet. The ram falls largely upon his horns, which are curved in such a way as to protect them from injury. The body rebounds slightly, and they get upon their feet as easily as if they had struck a pillow. At first the yearlings hesitate and almost lose their balance, but the mother makes them repeat the performance until they have accomplished it to her satisfaction.

"They are trained to leap chasms on all-fours, and finally the upward jump, which is a more difficult feat. If the height is not great they can clear it neatly, but if it is too high for that they will catch the rocky ledge with their fore-feet and pull themselves up like a man.

"In assisting their young to gain upper terraces they show much ingenuity. I once saw them make a ladder of their bodies. The biggest ram stood braced against the steep wall as high as his body could reach, head placed between his fore-feet, while the next biggest one rode his hind parts, and so on until the little ones could walk upon their broad backs to the top. We know that all animals make their young practise such feats as are necessary to their safety and advantage, and thus it is that these people are so well fitted to their peculiar mode of life.

"How often we are outwitted by the animals we hunt! The Great Mystery gives them this chance to save their lives by eluding the hunter, when they have no weapons of defence. The ewe has seen us, and she has doubtless warned all the clan of danger."

But there was one that she did not see. When the old chief left his clan to go to the secret place for chipping his horns, the place where many a past monarch of the Bad Lands has performed that painful operation, he did not intend to rejoin them immediately. It was customary with him at this time to seek solitude and sleep.

The two hunters found and carefully examined the tracks of the fleeing clan. The old ram was not among them. As they followed the trail along the terrace, they came to a leaping-place which did not appear to be generally used. Grayfoot stopped and kneeled down to examine the ground below.

"Ho!" he exclaimed; "the old chief has gone down this trail but has not returned. He is lying down near his chipping-place, if there is no other outlet."

Both men leaped to the next terrace below, and followed the secret pass into a rocky amphitheatre, opening out from the terrace upon which they had first seen the old ram. Here he lay asleep.

Wacootay pulled an arrow from his quiver.

"Yes," said his friend. "Shoot now! A warrior is always a warrior—and we are looking for horn for spoons."

The old chief awoke to behold the most dreaded hunter—man—upon the very threshold of his sanctuary. Wildly he sprang upward to gain the top of the cliff; but Wacootay was expert and quick in the use of his weapon. He had sent into his side a shaft that was deadly. The monarch's fore-hoofs caught the edge—he struggled bravely for a moment, then fell limp to the rocky floor.

"He is dead. My friend, the noblest of chiefs is dead!" exclaimed Grayfoot, as he stood over him, in great admiration and respect for the gray chieftain.

HOOTAY OF THE LITTLE ROSEBUD

On the south side of Scout Butte there is a crescent-shaped opening, walled in by the curving sides of the hill. This little plain cannot be seen from the top of the butte. There is a terrace upon its brow on which a few scrub pines grow, so regularly that one would think them set there by human hands. Half-way up the incline there stood at one time a lone cedar-tree, and at its foot there might have been discerned a flat, soft mound. It consisted of earth thrown up from the diggings of a cavern. The wild people approaching from the south could see this mound, but would scarcely note the entrance to the immense den hidden behind it. One coming down from the butte would not notice it, as there were no signs other than the earth pile. The Little Rosebud River takes its rise at the threshold of this natural barricade.

This was the home of Hootay, the aged medicine-man of the Little Rosebud country. He was a fighter of many battles, this great and wise grizzly, who was familiarly called Hootay, or Stubby Claws, by the Sioux hunters. They had all known of him for many years. It was believed of him that he had scalped not less than eight braves, and killed even more ponies and dogs. No less than three and ten times the Sioux had made expeditions against him, but each time they had failed. For this reason they declared that he had good war-medicine. Among the warriors it had long been understood that he who takes Hootay's scalp may wear a war-bonnet. This acknowledgment of his prowess, of course, was not made known to the aged yet still formidable bear.

Up and down the Little Rosebud he had left his well-known imprint, for he had lost two toes on one foot. Aside from the loss of his big claws, he had received several arrow and knife wounds during his warlike career.

Early in the fall, Hootay had felt a severe aching of his old hurts. He had eaten of every root-medicine that he knew, but there was no relief. Instinct led him to early retirement and hibernation.

His new home was a commodious one, well filled with dry grass and pine-needles. It is the custom of his people to remain quiet until the spring, unless serious danger threatens. A series of heavy storms in early winter had covered and concealed all his rakings of dry grass and other signs of his presence, therefore he thought himself secured from molestation. There he lay most of the time in a deep sleep.

. . .

The Sechangu Sioux never altogether leave this region. It is true that many wander away to the Missouri, the Muddy Water, or follow the buffalo down to the Platte River, but some would always rather trust to the winter hunt upon this familiar stream. This winter, High Head, with his little band of eleven men, was wintering at the old place. Among them was Zechah, a renowned hunter, who had followed this band because of his love for Hintola, the chief's daughter. It had been a long courtship, but they were married at last. Zechah's skill had been proved by his father-in-law, and the arrow test was only sport to him. His unerring aim was now the pride of the old chief.

The party encamped on the Little Rosebud had eaten all of their fresh meat. They must seek for game. Accordingly, three teepees went farther up the river. The winter was wellnigh over when there came a heavy thaw, and snow-shoes were made for the use of the hunters.

They pitched the teepees, looking like a trio of white conical bowlders, in a well-protected bottom. Winding gulches diverged from the main stream like the ribs of a huge snake, until they lost themselves in the hills. These dry creek-beds were sentinelled by cedar-trees, erect and soldier-like, which at a distance looked very black, but near by they appeared green.

The party was cheerful. High Head was in the best of

spirits, telling the history, traditions and legends of the region.

"This," said he, "is the country of the wild tribes who walk with four feet. It is the home of those people of unknown language. It has never been said that one could starve upon the Little Rosebud. In the summer it is the land of battles, both among the wild tribes and among men. In the winter-time there is peace."

At this moment a solitary singer, standing on the brink of a high cliff behind and above the teepees, broke into a weird and doleful chant.

"Listen to the warriors, the song of the warriors of Wazeyah, the god of cold and storm!" Thus he sang in a high, minor key, with sudden drops to lower notes and inflections.

When he ceased silence reigned, except for the occasional snapping of a burning ember.

Presently the watcher descended and made his report. "There is a great wind and snow coming. Our ponies are some distance away. We shall not be able to find them all for the darkness and the storm-wind approaching."

"Ho, ho," spoke High Head, confidently. "It is not bad. We shall eat meat to-morrow. The snow will be deep, and my son-in-law will have the easier hunting. It may be that I myself will lasso a great bear," chuckled the old man.

It snowed and the wind blew on that night and for four nights following. The little store of dried meat that they had brought with them was entirely exhausted. On the fifth day they all sat looking silently into the fire. Their faces were worn and haggard. The children cried for food, but there was no food. Wazeyah, the god of winter, still waged war, and the snow was piled high around their teepees.

Night came, the darkness fell heavily, and terrified them with the thought of death around their feeble fires. Famine was sitting among them with a stern face. At last all but two rolled themselves in their warm buffalo-robes and lay down. Even should the storm cease, they feared that none now was strong enough to hunt.

Zechah sat beside his young wife, gazing into the fire. "It will be sad news for my father that I died of starvation upon the Little Rosebud," he mused. "It will be told for generations to come, whenever they camp at this place."

When at last he lay noiselessly down, he could not sleep. Looking up through the smoke-hole, he sang a hunting song to himself in an undertone:

"The wind brings the secret news—good news of
   the hunting!
It is a scent—it may be a trail—it may be a sound
   of the game!
Whatever it be, it is a clew to the hunter,
A sign from above to appease hunger, to save
   life!"

Singing thus, Zechah had forgotten that he was

hungry, when all at once he saw a bright star through the smoke-hole. He had not noticed that the wind had ceased to blow.

The hunter arose softly, put on fur-lined moccasins, and girded himself with a strong strap over his lightest robe. He took his knife, a bow, and quiver full of arrows, and set out through the gray, frosty air.

It was now almost daylight. The rocks and pines were robed in white, like spirits. The snow was deep and heavy under Zechah's feet, but he was determined to succeed. He followed the ridges where the snow was well blown off. He had forgotten his own hunger and weakness, and thought only of the famishing people for him to serve.

Above the eastern hills the day was coming fast. The hunter hurried toward the gulches where he knew the game was wont to be. Just as he reached the higher ridges the sun appeared over the hills, and Zechah came upon the track of another early hunter. It was Shunkmanitoo, the gray wolf. He followed the trail until he came out upon a hill overlooking a deep gulch. He could only see the tips of the pines along its course. At a little distance, Shunkmanitoo sat upon his haunches, apparently awaiting Zechah. Again he took the lead and the wild hunter followed. The wolf looked back now and then as if to see whether the man were coming.

At last he paused upon a projecting bank commanding the bottom of the gulch. The Sioux approached him. When he had come very near, the wolf went on down the slope.

"Hi, hi!" Zechah spoke his thanks with arms outstretched toward the rising sun. Through a rift in the bank he saw a lone bison, ploughing up the deep snow in search of grass. He was well covered with snow and had not seen the two hunters appear above. Zechah at once dodged backward in order to approach his game behind cover and stealthily.

He was now almost over the gulch, partly concealed by a bunch of dead thistles. There was no suspicion in the mind of Tatanka. Zechah examined his arrows and bow. He placed the sharpest one to his bow-string, and with all the strength that he could muster he let the arrow fly. In another instant he saw Tatanka snort and plough up the snow like mad, with the arrow buried deep in his side. The bison did not know who or what had dealt him such a deadly thrust. He ran in a circle and fell upon the snow, while blood coursed from his nostrils, staining its whiteness.

Zechah was almost overcome by his good-fortune. Again he held his right hand outstretched toward the sun, and stood motionless.

"Hi, hi, hi, hi! tunkashela!" Thus he blessed the Father of all.

When the March thaw set in, the snow was melted off the south side of the hills. Hootay had doubtless had this danger in mind, for he could not have selected a more excellent place to avoid the catastrophe. But, alas! the best calculations will sometimes miscarry. It was nothing more than a stray root of the cedar-tree at his door which deviated the course of the water, running harmlessly down the hill, into Hootay's home. In a short time the old medicine-man was compelled to come out, drenching wet.

He sat down on a dry corner of the mound to meditate upon his future course. In his younger days he would have thought nothing of this misfortune, but now he was old and rheumatic. No inhabitant of that country knew better than he that it is not safe to sleep in the woods on the bottom-lands in the spring of the year. Hootay is a boastful hunter, often over-confident, yet wise in wood-craft, and what he has once learned he never forgets. He knew that when a thaw comes all the hills contribute their snow and water to the Little Rosebud, and for a few days it runs a mighty river. Even Chapa, the beaver, is wont at such times to use his utmost precautions to guard against disaster.

Hootay carefully considered the direction of the wind, sniffed the air to discover if any other wild hunter were near, and finally set out in a southwesterly direction toward the head of the Little Rosebud.

He had not gone far when he felt that he was scarcely equal to tramping through the slush and mud. More than this, he was leaving too broad a trail behind him. These considerations led him along the pine ridges, and for this course there was still another reason. He was hungry now, but there was little hope of meeting with any big game. Along the ridges there is early exposure of the ground where edible roots may be obtained, and where he hoped also to find dry bedding.

He had fair success in this, and had made himself somewhat comfortable when the blizzard set in. He had found tolerable shelter but very little food, and since his winter rest was so unexpectedly broken up, food he must have. As soon as the storm ceased, he had to venture out in search of it. He could no longer depend upon roots—the snow was far too deep for that. He must catch what he could. The old fellow was now almost hopelessly slow and weak, but he still had a good deal of confidence in himself.

He waded clumsily through the deep snow, following a dry creek-bed; and, now and then, from force of habit, he would stealthily climb the bank and scan the field above and below before exposing himself. This was partly for self-protection and partly in the hope of surprising his game.

Presently Hootay came upon the footprint of another hunter. He snarled and put his muzzle closer to the trail when he detected the hateful odor of man. At the same instant he smelled fresh meat.

The very smell seemed to give him a new lease of life, for he sat up on his haunches and began sniffing the air eloquently. His hair was as shaggy as that of an old buffalo-robe, and his age and sitting posture made his hump appear very prominent.

"Waugh, waugh!" the old man grunted, with an air

of disgust, for there came to his nose a strong human scent mingled with the savory odor of the life-giving meat.

Zechah distinctly heard the snort of a bear. He seized his bow and quiver full of arrows.

"Can it be that Hootay is near?" he muttered to himself. "He may perhaps add my scalp to the many that he has taken of my people, but I will first send an arrow of mine into his body!"

He rested his bow upon the shaggy head of the dead bull, and went on skinning it with a large knife, working rapidly. Presently the gray wolf approached from another direction.

"Ho, kola, you have guided me to game! It is yours and mine. You, too, shall have meat," he said.

As soon as he had skinned one side, Zechah cut off a generous piece and walked toward Shunkmanitoo, who was sitting upon his haunches, watching him work in that wonderful way with a single sharp thing in his hand. But he did not think it best to trust the wild man too far, for he still carried that sharp thing in his hand as he approached him with the meat. He arose and moved backward a few paces.

"Do not fear, kola! Warriors and hunters like ourselves must have faith in each other when they work together for a good cause," the Red man said, again. He placed the meat upon the snow where Shunkmanitoo had been sitting, and returned to his work.

After a time, and with apparent reluctance, the big,

burly wolf came back to his meat and examined it. At last he ate of it. It was good. He no longer feared the wild man. From time to time Zechah would throw him a piece of meat until he was satisfied.

The hunter had cleared away the snow around the buffalo, which was now cut up in convenient pieces for carrying. He was exceedingly hungry. He had, indeed, eaten a piece of the liver, which the Sioux always eats raw, but this only served to sharpen his appetite. He had heavy work before him, for he must take some of the meat home to his starving wife, and then bring as many of the people as were able to walk to carry the rest to camp. There were plenty of dry boughs of the pine. He made a fire by rubbing together the pieces of dry cedar-wood which every Indian hunter of that day carried with him, and, broiling strips of the savory meat upon live coals, he ate of it heartily.

Suddenly a fearful growl was heard. Zechah had dismissed the idea of a bear from his mind as soon as his friend Shunkmanitoo appeared. He was taken by surprise. When he looked up, Hootay was almost upon him. He came forward with his immense jaws wide open, his shaggy hair making him look as big as a buffalo bull against the clear whiteness of the landscape.

Shunkmanitoo's chance was small. He occupied the only road to Zechah's position, and there were perpendicular walls of snow on either side of him. His only hope lay in his quickness and agility. As Hootay rushed madly upon him with uplifted paw, the wolf sprang nimbly to one side and well up on the snow-bank. His assailant had to content himself with raking down the snow, and in the effort he plunged into a heavy drift from which he was unable to drag himself.

Hootay was in sad trouble, for he had tumbled right into a deep gully filled to the brim with soft snow, and the more he struggled the deeper he was sinking. Zechah perceived the situation, and made ready to send the fatal arrow.

Hootay waved his right paw pitifully. There was something human-like about him. The Indian's heart beat fast with excitement. Weakened by his long fast, he scarcely saw or heard clearly, but, according to the traditions of his people, the old bear addressed him in these words:

"No, Zechah, spare an old warrior's life! My spirit shall live again in you. You shall be henceforth the war prophet and medicine-man of your tribe. I will remain here, so that your people may know that you have conquered Hootay, the chief of the Little Rosebud country."

It is not certain that he really said this, but such was the belief of the hunter. He put his arrow back in the quiver, and immediately, according to custom, he took his pipe from his belt and smoked the pipe of peace.

A huge piece of meat was suspended from his shoulders above the quiver, and, with his bow firmly grasped in the right hand, Zechah addressed his friend Shunkmanitoo:

"Ho, kola, you have eaten what is yours; leave mine for my starving people!"

The wolf got up and trotted away as if he understood, while Zechah hurried back on his own trail with tidings of life and happiness.

He ran as often as he came to open ground, and in a short time stood upon the top of the hill with the little group of teepees just below him. The smoke from each arose sadly in a straight column, tapering upward until lost in the blue. Not a soul stirred and all was quiet as the dead.

"Ho, he ya hay!" the hunter chanted aloud, and ended with a war-whoop. Out of the sleepy-looking teepees there came a rush of men and women. Old High Head appeared with outstretched hands, singing and pouring forth praises. "Hi, hi, hi, hi!" he uttered his thanks, in a powerful voice, still stretching his arms to heaven.

Hintola was the quietest and most composed of them all. She went first to meet her husband, for it was the custom that, when the son-in-law returns with game, his wife must meet him outside the camp and bring back food to her parents.

Having distributed the meat in small pieces, High Head announced his son-in-law's success as a hunter, and solicited all who were able to join him in going after the remainder. He ended with a guttural song of cheer and gladness.

It was then Zechah told of his meeting with the other

wild hunters, and how Hootay was conquered and imprisoned in the snow.

"Ugh, ugh!" grunted High Head, with much satisfaction. "This means a war-bonnet for my son-in-law—a story for coming generations!"

But the hunter did not repeat the bear's words to himself until he had become a famous war prophet. When the people went after the meat, they found the old warrior lying dead without a wound, and with one accord they made a proper offering in his honor.

THE RIVER PEOPLE

Away up the Pipestone Creek, within sight of the Great Pipestone Quarry, lived old Chapawee and her old man Hezee, of the beaver tribe. Unlike some of their neighbors, they had emigrated from a great distance. They had, therefore, much valuable experience; and this experience was not theirs alone—it was shared with their immediate family. Hence their children and their children's children were uncommonly wise.

They had come to this country many years before, and had established their home in this ancient and much-prized resort of the two-legged tribe. Around the Pipestone Quarry the wild Red men would camp in large numbers every summer, and it seemed that the oldest beaver could not remember a time when they were not there. Their noisy ways were terrible indeed to the river people, who are a quiet folk.

It was the custom with this simple and hard-working pair to build a very warm house for themselves. In fact, they had both summer and winter homes, besides many supply and store houses. Their dam was always in perfect order, and their part of the creek was the deepest and clearest, therefore their robe of furs was of the finest. If any of the Hezee band was ever killed by the two-legs, their fur was highly valued.

Chapawee always insisted upon two rooms in her house: one for herself and the old man, and one for her yearling children who chose to remain with them for the first winter. She always built one very large house, running deep into the bank, so that in case of overflow or freshet they would still be safe. Besides the usual supply-houses, she and her old man excavated several dining-rooms. These are simply pockets underground at the edge of the stream. In case of any danger on the surface, they could take some food from a store-house and carry it to one of these dining-rooms, where it was eaten in peace.

It was the rule with the old folks to eat apart from their year-old children. The yearlings, on the other hand, eat all together, and have as much fun and freedom as they please. Their merriest frolics, however, are in the night, in and upon their swimming and diving pond. Here they coast rapidly head-first down a steep bank slippery with mud, lying upon their chests or sitting upon their haunches, and at times they even turn somersaults and perform other acrobatic feats. This coasting has a threefold object. It is for play and also for practice; to learn the art of sliding into deep water without unnecessary noise; and, more than all, according to the Red people, it is done for the purpose of polishing and beautifying their long, silky fur.

The beaver tribe are considered wisest of the smaller four-legged tribes, and they are a people of great common-sense. Even man gains wisdom and philosophy from a study of their customs and manners. It is in the long winter nights, as is believed and insisted upon by the wild Indians, that the beaver old folks recite their legends to their children and grandchildren. In this case it was usually Chapawee who related the traditions of her people and her own experiences, gathering about her all the yearlings and the newly married couples, who might take a notion to go off in search of a new claim, just as she and Hezee did. So it was well that they should thoroughly understand the ways and wisdom of their people.

To be sure, she had breathed it into them and fed them with it since before they could swim; yet she knew that some things do not remain in the blood. There are certain traits and instincts that are very strong in family and tribe, because they refer to conditions that never change; but other matters outside of these are likewise very useful in an emergency.

Old Chapawee could never sleep after the sun reaches the middle of the western sky in summer. In winter they all sleep pretty much all of the day. Having finished her supper with Hezee one night under the large elm-tree on the east side of the dam, she dove down with a somersault, glided along close to the bottom of the pond, inspecting every pebble and stray chip from their work-room, until she reached the assembly-room, which might almost be called a school-house in the manner of the paleface.

She came scrambling up the slippery bank to the middle entrance. No sooner had she shaken off the extra water from her long hair than Hezee's gray mustache emerged from the water, without exposing his head. He was teasing the old lady, trying to make her believe there was a crab in the landing. Quick as a flash she flopped over in the air and slapped the side of her broad tail upon the water where her spouse was lurking to deceive her. Down he dove to the bottom and lay there motion-less as if he expected her to hunt him up; but after a while he went off and notified all the young people that it was time for their gathering at the old meeting-house.

Here Chapawee occupied the place of honor, while Hezee filled the undignified position of errand-boy. All the young beavers came in, some still carrying a bit of sapling in their mouths, but, on realizing their mistake, each dove back to place it where it belonged. They arranged themselves in a circle, sitting upright on their flat tails for cushions, their hands folded under their chins.

"A long time ago," began Chapawee, the old beaver grandmother, "we lived on the other side of the Muddy Water (the Missouri), upon a stream called Wakpala

Shecha (Bad River). Father and mother, with my older brothers and sisters, built a fine dam and had a great pond there. But we led a hard life. There are not many ponds on Bad River and the stream dries up every summer, therefore thousands of buffalo came to our place to drink. They were very bad people. It seems that they do not respect the laws and customs of any other nation. They used to come by the hundred into our pond and trample down our houses and wear holes in the banking of our dam. They are so large and clumsy that they would put their feet right through the walls, and we had to hide in our deepest holes until we were very hungry, waiting for them to go away.

"Then there were the shunktokechas and shungelas (wolves and foxes), who follow the buffalo. They, too, are a bad and dangerous sort, so that mother and father had to be continually on the watch. We little beaver children played upon the dam only when mother thought it safe. In the night we used to enjoy our swimming, diving, and coasting school. We practised gnawing sticks, and the art of making mud cement that will hold water, how to go to the bottom silently, without effort, and to spank the water for a signal or danger-call with our tails.

"There were many other bad people in that country. There was the ugly old grizzly. He would sometimes come to our place to swim and cool off. We would not mind, only he is so treacherous. He was ready to kill one of us at any moment if we gave him the chance.

"Mother played a trick on him once, because he was

such a nuisance. He was wont to crawl out upon one of the logs which projected from the dam and over the deep water. This log was braced by posts in the water. Mother lay on the bottom and loosened the soil and then quickly pulled one of the posts away, and the old grizzly fell in headlong. She dove to one side, and, as the old man struggled to get out, crawled up behind him and gashed one of his hind paws with her sharp wood-choppers. Oh, how the old fellow howled and how he scrambled for the dam! He groaned long as he sat on the bank and doctored his wounded foot. After that he was never again seen to sit upon one of our logs, but when he came to the river to drink and cool off his hot paws he always took the farthest point from our houses, and then he only put one foot in the water at a time.

"Mother was dreadfully afraid of one wicked animal. That was Igmu, the mountain lion. He does not live in this part of the country, and it is such a relief," said the old beaver woman. "Whenever one of the Igmus comes to our place, we all hurry to deep water and lie there, for they have been known to dig through the walls of our houses.

"There was still another danger that our people had to contend with. Wakpala Shecha has a swift current and a narrow bed, and we had terrible freshets two or three times in a season.

"At last there came a great flood. It was after I was two years old and had learned everything—how to chop wood, which way to fell the trees, and what to store up for the winter; how to mix mud cement and drive posts in the creek bottom, and all of the other lessons. Early in the spring, while there was still snow on the ground, a heavy rain came. Every dry gulch was a torrent. We had never known such a flood. It carried away all our dams and made our strongest houses cave in. We did not dare to go to shore, for we could hear the wolves calling all along the banks.

"At last mother and father bound two drift-logs together with willow withes. We all helped, as none of us ever think of being idle. Upon the logs we made a rude nest, and here we all slept and ate as we floated down the stream.

"After several days we came to a heavily timbered bottom where there was a very large fallen tree. The roots held firmly to the bank and projected over the water. We all let go of our raft and climbed upon it; there were bushy branches at the top. We trimmed the trunk of the tree leading to dry land and built a temporary nest upon the bushy top, until the water should go down and we could find a good place to build. Mother and father went down the stream the next night to explore for a new home, and I was left in the nest with two brothers. We, too, explored the shores and little inlets near us, but we all came back to the nest that morning except mother and father. I have never seen them from that day to this.

"I and my two brothers slept together in the warm nest. All at once I felt a slight jar. I opened my eyes, and there lay upon the trunk of our tree a fierce Igmu, ready to fish us out with his strong arm and hooked claws.

"Kerchunk! I dropped into the deep stream to save my life. I swam a little way, and then came to the surface and peeped back. Ah, I saw him seize and violently dash one of my brothers against the tree, but the other I did not see. Perhaps he did as I did to save himself.

"I went down the Bad River until I came to the Big Muddy. Ice was floating in huge cakes upon the brown flood. I wanted to go, too, for I had heard of a country far to the sunrise of the great river. I climbed upon a floating ice-cake, and I moved on down the Muddy Water.

"I kept a close watch on the shores, hoping to see father and mother, but I saw no sign of them. I passed several islands, but the shores were loose sand. It was not the kind of soil in which our people build, so I did not stop, although there were fine tall cotton woods and all the kinds of trees that we eat. Besides, I did not care to go to shore or up the mouths of any of the creeks unless I should discover signs of our tribe. It was the first time in my life that I had ever been alone.

"So I kept on my ice-boat until I was out of food, and then I stopped at an island. I swam near the shore to find a good landing, and when I reached the bank I saw the footprints of a beaver man. My heart beat hard, and I could hardly believe my eyes. Some one had cut down a fresh sapling, and as I ate of the delicious bark and twigs

I was watching for him every moment. But he did not come.

"Then I went back to the water's edge to study the trail and see where he went. I found to my disappointment that he had gone back to the water. As my mother had taught me every beaver sign, I knew he was a traveller, come to take food, as I was. Hoping to overtake him, I hurried back to another floating cake of ice, and again I found myself going down the big stream.

"When I came in sight of another island, I watched carefully and saw some one moving on the shore. I was not hungry then, but I landed and began to nibble a twig at the water's edge. Presently I saw a beautiful young man coming toward me with a fine sapling in his mouth. I think I never saw a nicer looking beaver man than Kamdoka! He, too, was so glad to see me, and brought me the sapling to eat.

"We were soon so devoted and absorbed in each other that we forgot all about our journey. Kamdoka proposed that we should never leave one another, and I agreed. He at once built a rude house right under a high bank, where a tree had fallen over the water and its roots still held firm. On each side he planted double rows of sticks, and plastered the whole with mud. The narrow door was concealed by the tree-trunk, and led directly into the water. This was our first home. It was only for a few days, for we soon discovered that we could not live there.

"There were still a few large cakes of ice going down

the river, and on these we continued our journey, until one night our ice broke up and we were forced to swim. At last we came to a country which was just such as we would like to live in, and a stream that seemed the very one we had been dreaming about. It had good, firm banks, nice landings, and was just small enough to dam if necessary. Kamdoka and I were very happy. This stream the Red people call the Wakpaepakshan (Bend of the River).

"It was not long before the wild men came in great numbers to this beautiful river, and they were worse than Igmu and the grizzly. With their round iron with the iron strings they caught many of the beaver neighbors. Sometimes they would come with their dogs and drive us out of our houses with dry entrances; again, they would hide the round iron at our coasting and diving places, so that they caught many of our people. It is impossible to get away when one is bitten by one of these round irons. It was this which forced us at last to leave this lovely spot.

"While we still lived upon this stream, it came about that Kamdoka was called Hezee. His fine pair of wood-choppers had grown short and very yellow—that is why he is called Hezee—Yellow Teeth. Hezee and I forsook our home after our little Chapchincha was caught by the wild men. Hezee's sharp eyes discovered one of these ugly irons on our premises, and he reported it to me. I cautioned the children to be careful, and for a time they were so, but one morning my baby, my little Chapchincha, forgot, and, plunging blindly down from our landing, she was seized! They took her away with them, and the very next night we moved from that place.

"We found the mouth of this stream and followed it up. We selected many pretty places, but they were all claimed by some of the older inhabitants. Several times Hezee fought for the right to a home, and you can see where he had an ear bitten off in one of these fights. We had no peace until we came within sight of the Pipestone Quarry. To be sure, there are many wild men here also, but they come in midsummer, when they do not kill any beaver people. We simply keep close to our homes when they are here, and they scarcely ever trouble us.

"Children, we have made many fine homes, Hezee and I. We both came from beyond the Muddy Water—a very bad country. It is the country of coyotes, bears, bighorns, and the like. This is a country for our people. If any of you should be dissatisfied, or driven to leave your home, do not go beyond the Muddy Water. Always take one of the large streams, going to the south and the sunrise of the great river.

"You see my fingers getting stubby and nailless. Hezee's wood-choppers are no longer sharp. His long mustache is gray now. We are getting old. But we have lived happily, Hezee and I. We have raised many beaver people. We shall hope never to go away from this place.

"Children, be true to the customs of your people. Always have good homes. First of all, you must build a strong dam—then you will have deep water. You must have both underground homes and adobes. Have plenty of store-houses, well filled; and when the enemy comes to kill you, you can hold out for many days."

These were the old beaver woman's words to her young people. "Ho, ho!" they applauded her when she had done.

"You must learn all these things," said old Hezee, after his wife had done. "Always gnaw your tree more on the side toward the stream, so that it will fall over the water. You should cut down the trees on the very edge of the bank. Dive to the bottom and under the bank as the tree falls. Sometimes one of us is pinned down by a branch of a fallen tree and dies there. I myself have seen this. The water is the safest place. You must never go too far away from deep water."

Up and down Pipestone Creek for four or five miles spread the community formed by Chapawee's and Hezee's descendants. There was not any large timber, only a few scattered trees here and there, yet in most places there was plenty of food, for the river people do not depend entirely upon the bark of trees for their sustenance. No village was kept in better order than this one, for it was the wisdom of Chapawee and Hezee that made it so. Summer nights, the series of ponds was alive with their young folks in play and practice of the lessons in which the old pair had such a pride. Their stream overflowed with the purest of spring water. No fish were allowed to pollute their playgrounds. The river people do not eat fish, but no fish are found in their neighborhoods. If Mr. and Mrs. Otter, with their five or six roguish children, occasionally intruded upon their domain, the men of the tribe politely requested them to go elsewhere. So for a long time they held sway on the Pipestone Creek, and the little beaver children dove and swam undisturbed for many summers.

But Chapawee and Hezee were now very old. They occupied a pond to themselves. Both were half blind and toothless, but there were certain large weeds which were plentiful and afforded them delicious food. They remained in-doors a great deal of the time.

"Ho, koda!" was the greeting of two Indian men who appeared one day at the door of the old American Fur Company's store upon the Sioux reservation in Minnesota.

"How, Red Blanket! How, One Feather!" was the reply of the trader. "Isn't it about time for you people to start in on your fall trapping?"

"Yes, that is what we came for. We want traps, ammunition, and two spades on account. We have learned from the prairie Indians that the Big Sioux and its tributaries are full of beaver, otter, mink, and musk-rats. We shall go into that region for two months' hunting," said Red Blanket, speaking for the two. Both men were experienced trappers.

"We must strike the Pipestone Quarry and then follow down that stream to its mouth," remarked One Feather to his friend, after they had returned to camp with a load of goods that they had secured on credit, and had cut up some of the tobacco for smoking.

A few days later two solitary teepees stood on the shore of the pond, under the red cliffs of the Pipestone Quarry.

Red Blanket had gone down the stream to examine the signs. Toward evening, he came in with a large beaver on his shoulder.

"Koda, the stream is alive with beaver! I saw all of their dams and their houses, and many were out swimming without fear. They have not been disturbed in many years."

Soon both hunters emerged from their teepees heavily laden with traps, each man accompanied by his intelligent dog. They saw many fresh tracks of the inhabitants as they approached the beaver village. Their houses above ground were large and numerous, and their underground homes were as many, but the entrances were concealed by the water. The slides were still wet with recent plays.

"It is the home of their great chief," said Red Blanket, impressively. "Friend, let us sit down and offer the pipe! We must smoke to the beaver chief's spirit, that he may not cast an evil charm upon our hunting."

Both men sat down upon their crossed feet in the tall meadow-grass to carry out the familiar suggestion. One Feather pulled the leather tobacco-pouch from his hunting-belt, and filled the pipe. He held the mouth-piece to the four corners of the earth before handing it to his companion. As they smoked, their faces were serious, and expressed the full dignity and importance they had given to their intended massacre of a harmless and wise people.

"Let us go down a little way," said One Feather, finally. "I want to see how far the dams extend, and if it is only one family or many."

When they reached the second dam, the pond contained very little sign of beaver. There were landing and feeding places, but apparently they were not much used. The water was very deep and clear. Beyond this pond were many fresh signs again. This raised a new question in the minds of the Red hunters. On the way back again, they stopped on the shore of this pond and smoked again, while they discussed why there was not much life there, when there was such fine, deep, clear water, and the dams in such perfect condition.

"It may be a haunted pond," said One Feather.

"It is certain that some strange thing lives in this deep water," added Red Blanket, with gravity. They were fully concealed by the tall grass, and their dogs lay quietly at their sides.

"Look, my friend, it is he!" exclaimed One Feather, suddenly. They quickly faced about to behold an animal scramble up the steep bank. Both of his ears were entirely gone. The hair of his head and face was quite gray, including the few coarse whiskers that the beaver people wear. It looked very like the unshaven face of an old man. The hair of his body was short and rough—the silky, reddish coat was gone.

"It is an old, old beaver," whispered One Feather. "Ah, he is the grandfather of the village! I see now why this pond is not much used by the young folks. The old people live here."

He was apparently half blind and hard of hearing, as they had made enough noise to attract Hezee's attention, but he did not move. Soon Chapawee came up slowly and sat beside her old man. As the two sat there, upright, sunning themselves, there came from a distance an undertone call. Then a large female beaver glided up the stream, bearing in her mouth the fine, branchy bough of a tree, which she must have gone some miles to get. She approached the old pair, and kindly set the branch before them. While they greedily nibbled at it, the young woman quietly disappeared.

"These are people much like us. Surely they build much warmer houses than we do," said Red Blanket, laughing.

"Yes, they are a wonderful people," replied his friend, with a serious face. "This is the grandmother's pond. We shall respect it to-morrow," he continued. "We shall open the other dams and drain the water off, then the entrances will all be dry and our dogs will enter their homes and drive them out. When they come out, we shall spear them." This was the plan of One Feather, to which his companion assented.

It was a sad day for the river people. Presently the

two slayers came to the pond of Hezee and Chapawee, where they lay nestled together in their old, warm bed.

"I would like to leave the two old people alone," said One Feather. "But we cannot get at the upper ponds without draining this one." So it was decided to break down both of their dams. When the entrance to their house was exposed, the dogs rushed in and were beginning to bark, but One Feather called them back.

The work was accomplished, but it had taken two days. It was a sad massacre!

"We must repair the dam for the old folks before we go, and I have left four young ones alive, so that they can help feed them. I do not want their spirits to follow us," said One Feather. So on the very next morning the two hunters came back to the middle pond. Red Blanket with his dog was a little in advance.

"Come here, friend!" he called. There Hezee and Chapawee lay cold and stiff in the open.

They had gone out in the dark to rebuild their dam, according to the habit of a long life. Then they visited some of their children's homes for aid, but all were silent and in ruins. Again they came back to work, but it was all in vain. They were too old; their strength had left them; and who would care in such a case to survive the ruins of his house?

THE CHALLENGE

T he medicine-drum was struck with slow, monotonous beat—that sound which always comes forth from the council-lodge with an impressive air of authority. Upon this particular occasion it was merely a signal to open the ears of the people. It was the prelude to an announcement of the day's programme, including the names of those warriors who had been chosen to supply the governing body with food and tobacco during that day. These names were presently announced in a sing-song or chanting call which penetrated to the outskirts of the Indian village.

Just as Tawahinkpayota, or Many Arrows, was cutting up a large plug of black tobacco—for he was about to invite several intimate friends to his lodge—"Tawahink-payota, anpaytu lay woyutay watinkta mechecha, uyay yo-o-o!" the sonorous call, came for the second time. He stepped outside and held up an eagle feather tied to a staff. This was his answer, and signified his willingness to perform the service.

Having cut a sufficient quantity of tobacco, Many Arrows asked his wife to call at the home of each of the famous hunters whom he intended to honor, for it is the loved wife who has this privilege. Flying Bee was the first invited; then Black Hawk, Antler, and Charging Bear. The lodge of Many Arrows was soon the liveliest quarter of the Big Cat village—for this particular band of Sioux was known as the Big Cat band. All came to the host's great buffalo-skin teepee, from the top of which was flying a horse's tail trimmed with an eagle feather, to denote the home of a man of distinction.

"Ho, kola," greeted the host from his seat of dignified welcome. "Ho," replied each guest as he gracefully opened the door-flap. Inside of the spacious teepee were spread for seats the choicest robes of bear, elk, and bison. Mrs. Tawahinkpayota, who wished to do honor to her husband's guests, had dressed for the occasion. Her jet-black hair was smoothly combed and arranged in two long plaits over her shoulders. Her face was becomingly painted, and her superb garment, of richly embroidered doeskin completed a picture of prosperous matronhood.

While her husband offered the guests a short round of whiffs from the pipe of peace, she went quietly about her preparations for the repast, and presently served each in turn with the choicest delicacies their lodge afforded. When all with due deliberation had ended their meal, the host made his expected speech—for it was not without intention that he had brought these noted men together.

"Friends," said he "a thought has come to me strongly. I will open my mind to you. We should go to Upanokootay to shoot elk, deer, and antelope. We have been long upon the prairie, killing only buffalo. We need fine buckskin for garments of ceremony. We want also the skins of bears for robes suitable to a warrior's home, such as the home of each one of you. And then, you know, we must please our women, who greatly desire the elk's teeth for ornament, and for fine needle-work the quills of the porcupine."

"Ho, ho!" they replied, in chorus.

"It is always well," resumed Many Arrows, "for great hunters to go out in company. For this reason I have called you three together. Is it not true that Upanokootay, Elk Point, is the place we should seek?"

Again they all assented. So it came about that the five hunters and their wives, who must cure and dress the skins of the game, departed from the large camp upon the Big Sioux River and journeyed southward toward the favored hunting-ground.

It was near the close of the moon of black cherries, when elk and antelope roam in great herds, and the bears are happiest, because it is their feasting-time. There was to be a friendly contest in the hunting. All agreed to use no weapon save the bow and arrows, although the "mysterious iron" and gunpowder had already been introduced. Furthermore, they agreed that no pony should be used in running down the game. Thus the rules which should govern the character of the hunt were all determined upon in advance, and the natural rivalry between the hunters was to be displayed in a fair and open trial of skill and endurance. It was well known that these five were all tried and mighty men beyond most of their fellows. This does not mean that they were large men; on the contrary, none was much above the medium height, but they were exceptionally symmetrical and deep-chested.

On the second morning, the men scattered as usual, after selecting a camping-ground at which all would meet later in the day. Each hunter was attired in his lightest buckskin leggings and a good running pair of moccasins, while only a quiver with the arrows and bows swung over his stalwart shoulders. All set out apparently in different directions, but they nevertheless kept a close watch upon one another, for the chief occasion of an Indian's mirth is his friend's mistakes or mishaps in the chase.

Flying Bee hastened along the upper ridges overlooking the plain. What! a great herd of elk grazing not far away! It was needful to get as close to them as possible in order to make a successful chase. He threw off all superfluous garments, tossed his quiver to one side, and took three arrows with the bow in his hand. He then crept up a ravine until he came within a short distance of the herd. As he cautiously raised his head for a survey, he saw a jack-rabbit's long ears a little way off, while a yearling antelope showed itself above the long grass to the left.

"Ugh, you may fool the elk, but you can't fool me!" he remarked as he smiled to himself.

Again, on the farther side, a fawn's head was turned in the direction of the herd.

"Ho, ho!" chuckled Flying Bee. "Where is the other?"

Just then, at his right, a little buffalo calf's head was pushed cautiously above a bunch of grass.

"Ugh, you are all here, are you? Then I will show you how to chase the elk."

He pulled a large bunch-weed and held it in front of him so that the elk could not see him for a moment. Then he ran forward rapidly under cover of the weed.

He had scarcely done this when Charging Bear emerged from the direction of the fawn display. Tawahinkpayota came forth from the antelope head, while Black Hawk and Antler rose up where the jack-rabbit and calf had lain. Bee disappeared in the midst of the fleeing herd, as he was a runner of exceptional swiftness. The great herd departed in a thunder of hoofs, and the five friends paused to smoke together and exchange jokes before going to examine their game. Black Hawk, whose quarry had gone with the rest, carrying his arrows, was greatly disappointed, and he immediately became a butt for the wit and ridicule of the others.

"How is this, friend? Have the elk such a fear of the harmless jack-rabbit? It seems that they did not give you a chance to make your swift arrows count."

"Ha, ha, ha!" laughed Tawahinkpayota. "The elk people never knew before that a rabbit would venture to give them chase."

"Ah, but he has often been seen to run after elk, deer, and even buffalo to save his own scalp from the wolves when he is pursued!" Thus Charging Bear came to the rescue of his friend.

And so they joked while Antler filled the pipe.

"We must take only one or two short whiffs," he reminded them, as he crowded down the mixture of tobacco and willow bark into the red bowl. It was the time of hunting and running, when men do not smoke much, and the young men not at all.

Having finished their smoke, they arose and followed the trail of the elk. The animal shot by Flying Bee lay dead not far away, with an arrow sticking out of the opposite side of its body, for he was a powerful man. Soon they came to two does lying dead, but there were no arrows, and the wounds were not arrow wounds.

"Ho, kola, hun-hun-hay! Surely you could not use your knife while running bow in hand?" remarked Black Hawk.

"We shall make it a rule hereafter that no one shall use any strange or unusual weapon," added Many Arrows, jestingly.

"You see now how a Bee can sting!" chimed in Charging Bear, in much mirth and admiration for the feat of his friend.

This, or something not unlike it, was now their daily experience, while their wives busily dressed the skins of their game and cured such of the meat as they cared to save. Each man kept a mental record of his shots for future reference, and all bore with unfailing good-humor the kindly ridicule of their fellows. They often hunted singly, yet the tendency was to be on the lookout for one another as well as for themselves, knowing that they were always in more or less peril from ferocious animals, as well as from the enemies of their people. They would also send out one of their number from time to time to scout the ground over which they expected to hunt on the following day.

"Ho, koowah yay yo, kola!" was the cry of Black Hawk, one evening, inviting his companion hunters to feast at his lodge. He had been appointed to scout the field south of their camp, and, having explored the country thoroughly, was ready to make his report.

"The land south of us, along the river," said he, "is well peopled with elk, deer, and beaver, and the prairie adjoining is full of buffalo. As far as the eye can see, their herds are countless. But, friends," he added, "there are also bears in this region. I have seen them, and I saw many of their fresh tracks."

Black Hawk was a clever scout, and could imitate both the actions and call of any animal so as almost to deceive his fellow-hunters. He had covered considerable ground that afternoon.

"There is, however, no recent sign of any of our

enemies, and the game is better than in any year that I have come here," he said again.

"Ho, ho, ho!" was the chorus of thanks from the others.

"Flying Bee, you have hunted in this region longer than the rest of us. Tell us of the wisdom of other years," suggested one.

"Ho, kola, hechetu!" again came the approving chorus.

The feast was eaten, the pipe was laid aside, and Flying Bee began thus:

"It was in the same year that the great battle was fought between the Omahas and the Yankton Sioux, under this high ridge. We were hunting upon the other side, and I saw then as many elk and deer as there are now. I was a young man and had just begun to know the ways of the elk and his weaknesses.

"You must never allow him to get your scent, but you can let him see you, provided he does not understand. If he thinks you are some other animal, he will not trouble to move away, but if you make him curious he will come to you. If you put on a brown suit and appear and disappear in the edge of the woods at evening or early morning, the doe will approach you curiously. In the spring moons you can deceive her with the doe-caller, and a little later than this you can deceive her with the call of the buck elk.

"If you have a 'mysterious iron' you can shoot down any number of them. A woman or a white man could do as much. Also, if you have a swift pony you can run down almost any game. This is no true test of skill. Do as we are doing now—hunt on foot with only the bow and arrow or the knife and stone for weapons, for these were the weapons of our people for untold years.

"There are no finer animals than the elk folk. I have studied their ways, because, as you know, we have followed their customs in courtship and warfare as much as those of any nation. Doubtless all our manners and customs were first copied from the ways of the best animal people," added the speaker.

"Ho, kola, hechetu!" was the unanimous endorsement of his friends.

"From now on the great elk chieftain gathers his herd. The smaller herds are kept by smaller chiefs, and there are many duels. I say again, no duel is brave and honest as that of the elk. When the challenge comes, it means a death-notice and must be accepted. The elk is no coward; he never refuses, although he knows that one at least must die in the fight.

"The elk woman, too, is the most truly coquettish of all animals. She is pretty and graceful, but she is ready to elope with the first suitor. Therefore, we call the young man who is especially successful in courtship the elk young man. The girlish and coquettish young woman we call the elk maiden.

"The bear and the buffalo are people of much mouth. They make a great deal of noise when they fight. The elk is always silent and does nothing that is unbecoming. Those others are something like the white men, who curse and broil much among one another," Bee concluded, with an air of triumph.

"I have several times witnessed a combat between the elk and the grizzly. I have also seen the battle between the buffalo bull and the elk, and victory is usually with the latter, although I have known him to be mortally wounded."

"And I have witnessed many times the duels between great elk chiefs," joined in Many Arrows.

"These people go in large bands from this time until the winter, when they scatter in smaller bands. The elk leads a bachelor's life from January until midsummer, and about July he begins to look for company." This was Antler's observation.

"There are two large herds near Smoky Hill, upon the river meadows. It will be easy to catch some of the does in the evening, when they return to their fawns. They hide the fawns well.

"Some leave them in the woods, others take them into the deep ravines. My wife is anxious that I should bring her a fawn's skin for a fancy bag," suggested Black Hawk.

"It will take some good running to catch a fawn at this time of the year. They are quite large now, and the earliest fawns are already out with the herds," remarked Many Arrows. "The moon of strawberries is really the best time to catch the doe and fawn with a birchen whistle. However, there are some still hidden, and as long as the doe suckles her fawn she will always come back to it at evening."

Having received such encouraging reports from their advance scout, the wild hunters immediately removed their camp to the vicinity of the great herd. It was a glorious September morning, and the men all left for the field at daybreak to steal upon the game. They hurried along in single file until near enough, then they broke ranks, separated, and crept around an immense herd of elk. The river here made a quick turn, forming a complete semicircle. A lovely plain was bounded by the stream, and at each end of the curve the river and woods met the side of the upper plateau. The whole scene was commanded by the highest point of the ridge, called by the Indians Smoky Hill.

The elk people had now reached the climax of their summer gayety and love-making. Each herd was ruled by a polygamous monarch of the plains—a great chieftain elk! Not a doe dared to leave the outskirts of the herd, nor could the younger bucks venture to face their mighty rival of the many-branched horns and the experience of half a score of seasons.

Of this particular herd the ruler was truly a noble monarch. He had all the majesty that we might expect of one who had become the master of a thousand does.

The elk women were in their best attire and their happiest spirits. The fawns were now big enough to graze and no longer dependent upon their mothers' milk, therefore the mothers had given themselves over wholly to social conquests. Every doe was on the alert, and used her keen sight, ear, and scent to the utmost to discover the handsomest elk young man, who, though not permitted to show himself within the kingdom of the monarch, might warily approach its boundaries.

Hehaka, the monarch, was dressed in his finest coat and had but lately rubbed the velvet from his huge and branchy antlers. His blood was richest and bluest of the elk folk. He stood upon the outer edge and continually circled the entire herd—a faithful guardian and watchful of his rights.

Around this herd the wild hunters converged and, each taking up his assigned position, were ready to begin the attack. But they delayed long, because of their great admiration for the elk chieftain. His bearing was magnificent. The unseen spectators noted his every movement, and observed with interest the behavior of the elk women.

Now and then a doe would start for the edge of the woods, and the ruler would have to run after her to remind her of his claim. Whenever this happened, a close scrutiny would reveal that a young buck elk had shown his broadside there for a moment, desiring to entice one of the monarch's elk women away. These young bucks do not offer a challenge; they dare not fight, for that would mean certain death; so that they show the better part of valor in avoiding the eye of the jealous monarch. But they exert the greatest attraction over the susceptible elk women. All they need do is to show themselves, and the does will run towards them. So the Indians say of certain young men, "He has a good elk medicine, for he is always fortunate in courtship."

About the middle or end of August these young bucks begin to call. They travel singly over hill and plain, calling for their mates until their voices grow hoarse and fail utterly. All this finally ends in the breaking-up of the monarch's harem.

The call of the elk when new is a high-pitched whistle, pleasant to hear as well as fascinating and full of pathos. The love-call of the Indian youth is modelled upon the whistle of the elk.

Now, the Yanktons, unknown to our party, had routed a large herd of elk on the day before on the plains south of the high ridge, but the great chieftain of the herd had escaped into the hills.

His herd destroyed, the chief was all alone. He could not forget the disaster that had befallen his people. He came out upon the highest point of the ridge and surveyed the plains below—the succession of beautiful hills and valleys where he had roamed as lord. Now he saw nothing there except that immediately below him, upon a grassy plateau, were one or two circular rows of the white, egg-shaped homes of those dreadful wild men who had destroyed or scattered all his elk women. He snorted and sniffed the air and tossed his immense horns, maddened by this humiliation.

"It is now calling-time. I have acquired the largest number of branches on my horns. It is my right to meet any king among my people who thinks himself better able than I to gather and keep a harem." Though weary and disappointed, he now grew bold and determined. "It is now calling-time," he seemed to say to himself. "To-morrow at sunrise my voice shall open the call upon the old elk hill! I know that there must be many elk women not far away. If any buck should desire to meet me in battle, I am ready!"

The lonely elk passed a wretched night. He could not forget what had happened on the day before. At dawn hunger seized him, and he ate of the fine dew-moistened grass until he was satisfied. Then he followed the oak ridges along the side of Smoky Hill, travelling faster as the day began to break. He thought he saw here and there a herd of elk women loom large through the misty air, but as the shadows vanished he discovered his mistake. At last he stood upon the summit, facing the sunrise.

The plains below were speckled far and wide with herds of antelope and of bison. The Big Sioux River lazily wound its way through the beautiful elk land. He saw five teepees upon a rich plain almost surrounded by a bend of the river, and not far away there grazed a great band of elk women, herded apparently by a noble buck.

The heart of the lonely one leaped with gladness, and then stung him with grief and shame. He had not heard one elk-call that year as yet. It was time. Some-thing told him so. It would not break the elk's custom if he should call.

His blood arose. His eyes sparkled and nostrils dilated. He tossed his branchy, mighty antlers and shook them in the air, he hardly knew why, except that it was his way of saying, "I dare any one to face me!"

He trotted upon the very top of Smoky Hill. The air was fresh and full of life. He forgot at that moment everything that had passed since his mother left him, and his mind was wholly upon the elk people who were gathered there below him in a glorious band. He felt that he must now call, and that his voice should sound the beginning of the elk-calling of that season upon the Big Sioux.

Flying Bee had notified his fellow-hunters by means of a small mirror of the presence of a grizzly in their midst, and each one was on the alert. Soon all had located him, and moved to a point of safety. They preferred to see him attack the herd rather than one of themselves, and they were certain that the monarch of the Big Sioux would give him a pitched battle. He was the protector of every doe in his band, and he had doubtless assured them of that when he took them into the herd.

"Whoo-o-o-o!" a long, clear whistle dropped apparently out of the blue sky. A wonderful wave of excitement passed through the great herd. Every tobacco-leaf-shaped ear was quickly cast toward Smoky Hill. The monarch at once accepted the challenge. He stepped in front of his elk women and lifted his immense head high up to sniff the morning air. Soon he began to paw and throw up the earth with his fore and hind hoofs alternately.

Just then the second call came—a piercing and wonderful love-call! The whole band of elk women started in the direction of the challenger. Every one of them gave the doe's response, and the air was filled with their stamping and calling.

The monarch started to intercept them in great rage and madness. The hunters all ran for the nearest tall trees from which they might witness the pending duel, for they knew well that when two of these rulers of the wilderness meet at this season it can be for nothing less than a battle to death. As Bee settled himself among the boughs of a large ash that stood well up on the brow of the river-bank, he easily commanded the scene.

He saw the challenger standing upon the highest point of Smoky Hill. In a moment he descended the slope and ran swiftly to the level of the plain. Here he paused to give the third challenge and the love-call—the call that the Indian youth adopted and made their own.

Again the elk women were excited and stamped their hoofs. The monarch now let them alone, and started on a run to meet the challenger. Bee could not restrain himself; he had to give a sympathetic whoop or two, in which his fellows willingly joined. The elk paid no attention, but when old grizzly found that he was among many warriors, he retreated to an adjoining creek to hide.

The challenger saw his adversary coming, and he hurried forward without a pause. The elk women were thrown into the greatest confusion, and even the five

170

warrior-hunters became much excited, for they always admired a brave act, whether the performer were a man like themselves or one of the four-footed folk.

When the monarch saw that the challenger was in earnest, he took up his position in front of his herd. On came the other, never pausing after the third call. When he was within a hundred paces, the monarch again advanced, and the two came together with a great clash of mighty antlers. Both trembled violently for an instant; then each became tense in every muscle of his body as they went into action.

Now one was pushed bodily along for some distance, and now the other was pressed back. At one time both kneeled down and held each other fast with locked horns. Again they were up and tugging with all their strength. The elk women were excitedly calling and stamping in a circle around their lovers and champions, who paid no heed to them.

At last the monarch made a rush with all the strength that was left him. He turned the body of the challenger half-way round. Quick as a flash he pulled off and jabbed three prongs of his horns deep into the other's side. But, alas! at that moment he received an equal wound in his own body. Exhausted by loss of blood, they soon abandoned the contest. Each walked a few steps in an opposite direction, and lay down, never to rise again!

All of the hunters now descended and hurried to the spot, while the elk women fled in a great thunder of hoofs. They wished to give to the two combatants a warrior's homage.

The challenger was already dead. The monarch was still living, but his life was ebbing so fast that he did not even notice their approach.

Flying Bee held his filled pipe toward the fallen king. "Let thy spirit partake of this smoke, Hehaka!" he exclaimed. "May I have thy courage and strength when I meet my enemy in battle!"

It is the belief of the Indian that many a brave warrior has the spirit of a noble animal working in him.

The five hunters were so greatly touched by this event that they returned to camp empty-handed out of respect for the brave dead. They left handfuls of cut tobacco beside each of the elk, and Black Hawk took off one of the two eagle feathers that he always wore and tied it to the monarch's head.

WILD ANIMALS FROM THE INDIAN STAND-POINT

T ula, tula, kola, the game is plentiful—once
more the flats of the Cheyenne are covered
with buffalo—winter is still at a distance and
all is well!"

Thus laughingly exclaimed old Hohay as he
approached the teepee of Sheyaka, a renowned hunter
of the Sioux.

"Ugh, you are all here, even Kangee and Katola.
What is in your minds?" he continued, as he entered and
took his seat.

"Ho, brother-in-law, it is good of you to join us. We
are merely enjoying our smoke," replied the genial host.
"Ah, you are still the coyote that you were in your
younger days! Smoke never entered your nostrils without
drawing you as by a rope. But now that you are here you
must decide between us. Kangee maintains that the doe
never fights. I have said that she has been known to

defend herself even more fiercely than her brother," urged Sheyaka.

"It is agreed by all our hunters that you have studied the ways of the animals more closely than any of us," chimed in Kangee. "Of course, we have all heard the traditions of the old hunters as they have been handed down from our fathers, but the things that we ourselves have seen and known are straight and strong in our minds as a newly made arrow," he added.

Hohay had been pulling silently at his long-stemmed pipe, but in a minute he passed the pipe on to Kangee and tightened the robe about his knees to get himself into a story-teller's attitude, for he had no idea of dismissing this favorite subject in a few words.

"We must remember," he began, slowly, "that the four-footed people do not speak after our fashion. But what of that? Do we not talk with our eyes, lips, fingers? Love is made and murder done by the wink of an eye or by a single motion of the hand. Even we ourselves do not depend altogether upon speech for our communication with one another. Who can say that they have not a language?"

"Ho, ho, henaka," interrupted Kangee. "I will help you a little here, good Hohay! It is well known that the alarm-call of the loon, the crane, and the wild goose is understood by all of the winged people that swim the lakes. This is not all. Many of the four-footed people of the woods know it as well. It often happens when I hunt water-fowl that one gives the alarm and immediately all the ducks will swim out, away from the shore. Those that cannot swim crouch down to conceal themselves, and even small animals stealthily and swiftly dodge back into the woods. Yet the same birds' love and play calls were not heeded nor did they disturb the peace, although they were at times very noisy and talkative."

"Ho, ho," they all said.

"Tadota and I," continued Kangee, "once saw a doe call to her fawn to lie down and hide. It happened in this way. We were hunting up a ravine and came upon the doe and fawn about a hundred paces apart. They were both standing to graze, as it was early in the evening. As soon as the doe saw us she gave her warning call, which usually causes the fawn to run toward her. But in this case the little creature dropped instantly into the tall grass. After we had shot the doe we came up to her, but she lay perfectly still and refused to rise. I may be wrong, but I believe the doe told the fawn to drop.

"I have also seen a doe and fawn playing," he went on, "when plainly the mother directed her young to leap a stream which she herself had just crossed. The fawn was timid and would not jump. Three times the doe called, pounding the ground with her fore-foot. At last she sprang back and caressed the fawn with her nose and stood with her a little while, and then once more leaped the stream. The young fawn came to the very edge of the bank and nervously smelled and examined it. Meanwhile the doe called emphatically, and finally the little one jumped. So I think there is good ground for saying that the wild animals have a language to which we have not the key."

"Kangee is right," spoke up Sheyaka.

"Ugh," said Katola, who had not spoken before. "He has made the doe and fawn real people. They can neither speak nor reason," added the doubter, "and the fawn hides because it is its nature to hide, not because the mother has instructed it."

"Hun-hun-hay!" exclaimed Hohay, who was older than the other three. "The animals do teach their young, and the proof is that the young often fail to perform the commonest acts of their parents when captured very early and kept by man. It is common knowledge among us that the buffalo calf and fawn have refused to swim when tamed, and do not run swiftly and well as when trained by the mother, and, in fact, have no disposition to run when let loose with the prairie before them.

"Again, it is well known that all elk are not equally good runners. Some of them we could run down on foot and that shortly, while others try the strength of the best running horse, all in the same season of the year and even in the same herd. It looks to me as if some mothers were better trainers than others.

"This training is very important, because wild life is a constant warfare, and their lives often depend upon their speed in flight. The meat-eating animals, too, must be in good trim, as they are compelled to chase their game daily.

"The bear is one of the hardest trainers among the

wild mothers. In the midsummer moon she gives them a regular trial-heat. It is an unlimited run, only measured by the endurance of the mother. The poor cubs drop out of the race one by one, whenever one is winded. But in case one holds out, he remains with her in the same den during the following winter. That is the prize of the victor."

"Who has seen or killed the mother-bear in the winter with a single cub?" asked Katola.

"I have seen it," replied Hohay.

"And I also," added Sheyaka.

"But I still do not believe that they teach their young, like the Red people," Katola said. "Some run better than others because they are stronger, not because of their better training."

"Sheyaka wants to hear about the doe," resumed Hohay, "but I have talked much on other points so as to get my mind fairly on the trail. The doe is the most sensitive animal of all that man hunts. She is the woman in every way, depending upon her quickness and cunning in hiding and the turns she takes in her flight. Perhaps she has the best nose and ears of all animals, but she has a very small idea of the hunter's acuteness. She knows well the animal hunters, who can smell and run, but of man she knows little, except that, though clumsy, he is dangerous.

"This delicate little squaw can fight desperately when she is cornered or in defence of her young. She has even been known to attempt the life of a man under those circumstances! But, Sheyaka, it is time to smoke," said the wild philosopher at this point.

"Ho, koda, chandee ota," replied Sheyaka, as he graciously produced the finely cut tobacco and willow bark. "Katola, you have a good voice; sing us a hunting song," added the good-natured host.

"Ho, ho," the company spoke in approval of the suggestion.

Katola gave them a song without words, the musical, high-pitched syllables forming a simple minor cadence, and ending with a trill. There was a sort of chorus, in which all the men joined, while Katola kept time with two sticks, striking one against the other, and Washaka, the little son of the host, danced in front of them around the embers of the central fire. The song finished, the pipe was silently smoked, passed and re-passed around the circle.

At last old Hohay laid it aside, and struck a dignified attitude, ready to give the rest of his story.

"Katola is right in one way," he admitted. "He cannot be blamed for having never seen what has been witnessed by other hunters. We believe what we ourselves see, and we are guided by our own reason and not that of another. Stop me when I tell you a thing hard to believe. I may know it to be true, but I cannot compel you to believe it."

Kangee could not contain himself any longer, but exclaimed:

"I have even known the coyote to make her pups

carry and pile the bones of the buffalo away from their den!"

"Ugh, ugh!" responded the old man. "You compel me to join Katola. That is hard to prove, and while the coyote is a good trainer and orderly, and it is true that their old bones are sometimes found outside the den, I have never before heard that she makes the little ones pile them. I am not willing to put that into my bag of stories.

"Now, as to the ability of the doe to fight. When I was a boy, I hunted much with my father. He was a good coyote—he trained well and early. One spring we were living in the woods where there was very little game, and had nothing to eat but musk-rats. My father took me with him on a long deer-hunt. We found a deer-lick beside a swollen pond. The ground was soft around the pond, with reeds and rushes.

"'Here we shall wait,' said my father.

"We lay concealed in the edge of the woods facing a deer-path opposite. In a little while a doe appeared on the trail. We saw that she was in full flight, for her tongue was protruding and she breathed hard. She immediately waded out to the middle of the pond and stood with only her head out of water.

"On her trail a large gray wolf came running, followed by his mate. The first, without hesitation, swam out to the doe. She reared upon her hind-feet as he approached, raising both of her front hoofs above the water. The wolf came on with mouth wide open and grinning rows of teeth to catch her tender throat, but her pointed hoofs struck his head again and again, so rapidly that we could not count the blows, which sounded like a war-club striking against a rock. The wolf disappeared under the water.

"Just at this moment the other wolf emerged from the rushes and hastened to the assistance of her mate. The doe looked harmless, and she swam up to her. But the same blows were given to her, and she, too, disappeared. In a little while two furry things floated upon the surface of the pond.

"My father could not restrain his admiration for her brave act; he gave a war-whoop, and I joined him heartily."

"Ho, ho! You did not shoot the doe, did you?" they asked.

"If we did that, we would be cowards," replied the story-teller. "We let her go free, although we were in need of food. It was then I knew for the first time that even the doe while in flight watches every chance to make a good defence. She was helpless on dry land, so she deliberately awaited the wolves in the deep water, where she could overcome them. Thereafter, when I hunt I keep this in my mind. My game is fully awake to the situation, and I must use my best efforts and all my wits to get him. They think, and think well, too."

"It is all true," Kangee assented, enthusiastically. "The buffalo is the wisest of all the larger four-footed people," he went on, "in training the young calf."

"Ugh, ugh! they do not train their young, I tell you!" interrupted Katola, again.

"Wait until Kangee tells what he knows and then tell us your thought," interposed Hohay. "It is not fair to doubt the word of a fellow-hunter."

"I want to tell what I myself saw," resumed Kangee. "Near the Black Hills, in the early spring, we hunted the bison. My brother and I followed two cows with their small calves. They disappeared over a ridge into a deep valley.

"We hastened on and saw only one cow running on the other side without her calf. In the ravine we came upon the other, and saw her vigorously push the calf down two or three times, but each time it rose again."

"Ha, ha, ha! The calf refused to hide," they all laughed.

"When she saw us, she turned and ran on with her calf. Presently she entered another valley, and emerged on the other side without the little one. At the first ravine, one cow succeeded in cachêing her calf—the other failed. She had a disobedient child, but finally she got rid of it. After a time the calf understands its mother's wishes; then she always succeeds in cachêing her young when pursued."

"Tula, tula, kola! That is common knowledge of all hunters; surely Katola cannot doubt that," remarked Hohay.

"Not that—I only said that they do not teach them.

They do these things without thought or deliberate planning," insisted Katola.

"But you must know that even a baby who has no mother after a while forgets to take the breast when one is offered to him. It is constant bringing to the young creature and continual practice—that is teaching," Hohay declared, and the other two nodded approval.

"Neither do I believe in a language of animals," Katola remarked.

"It may be there is none; but, even so, do we not convey the strongest meaning without a sound or a word? In all our speeches what is most important may be expressed by a silence, a look, or a gesture—even by the attitude of the body." Hohay continued rapidly in his argument: "Is it impossible that these people might have a simple language, and yet sufficient for their use?

"All that a man can show for his ancestry, when he is left alone from infancy, are his two legs, two arms, a round head, and an upright carriage, or partially upright. We know this from those children who have been found by wolves and nourished in their caves until well grown. They were like beasts and without a language.

"It is teaching that keeps man truly man and keeps up the habits and practices of his ancestors. It is even so with the animals. They, too, depend for their proper skill and development upon the mother influence, encouragement, and warning, the example constantly set before them which leads them to emulate and even surpass their elders. We Red men have no books nor do we build houses for schools, as the palefaces do. We are like the bear, the beaver, the deer, who teach by example and action and experience. How is it? Am I right?" the old man appealed to his attentive listeners.

"Yes, yes, it is true," replied Kangee and Sheyaka, but Katola said nothing.

"Is it not our common experience," resumed Hohay, "that when we kill or trap one or two beaver in a night, all the beaver stay in-doors for several nights within a considerable distance? This is equally true in the case of the otter and mink. I have often started up a deer, and every deer he passed in his flight would also flee. But when they run at random in play they do not cause a general stampede.

"Their understanding of one another's actions is keener and quicker than we can give news by words, for some are always doubters, and then we of the two-legged tribe are given to lie at times, either with or without intention. This proves that the animal does not lack the power to give news or intelligence to his family and neighbors. If this is so, then they do not lack means to convey their wishes to their young, which is to teach them."

This declaration was received in silence, and, presently, Hohay added: "How is it, Sheyaka? Is it commonly accepted by our hunters that some of the four-footed people play tag and hide-and-seek with their little ones?"

"Ho, it is well known," responded the host. "I have seen a black-tail doe run away from her fawn and hide.

When the little one ran to find her, calling as he seeks, she would rush upon him playfully at last from some unexpected nook or clump of bushes."

"Once I saw a beaver," continued Hohay, "send her whole family to the opposite side of the pond when she was about to fell a large tree. One of the young ones was disobedient and insisted upon following the mother to her work, and he was roundly rebuked. The little fellow was chased back to the pond, and when he dove down the mother dove after him. They both came out near the shore on the opposite side. There she emphatically slapped the water with her tail and dove back again. I understood her wishes well, although I am not a beaver."

"It is the way of the beaver," remarked Sheyaka, "not to allow her children to play out-of-doors promiscuously or expose themselves to danger. She does not take them with her to fell trees until they are old enough to look out for themselves. But she brings them all out at night to learn the mother-tricks and trade. She is perhaps the wisest of all the smaller animals."

"The grizzly is an excellent mother of her kind," suggested Kangee. "I once followed a mother bear with two small cubs. As soon as she discovered me, she hastened toward a creek heavily fringed with buffalo-berry bushes. When she disappeared over the bank, I hurriedly followed to see what she would do. She had sent one of the cubs into the thick bushes, and a little farther on she tried to dispose of the other in another good place, but the cub would not obey. It came out each time and followed her. Suddenly she grabbed and threw it violently into a thicket and then ran around the creek and came out almost opposite. There she watched me from under cover."

"Bears, wolves, and foxes," commented old Hohay, "often cuff or slap their young to teach them obedience. Katola might say that the obedience is inborn or instinctive, but it is not. Young animals can be very rude and disobedient to their parents when they are small, but their mothers' training is strict and is continued until they leave them. We Red people have followed their example. We teach our children to respect and obey their elders," concluded the old story-teller.

"The fox is a most orderly eater," Kangee remarked. "Why, she will not allow her children to eat greedily! We know that when she finds a nest full of ducks' eggs—for she is a great egg-stealer—she will drive away the excited young foxes, and roll out egg after egg to each one in turn. Each must wait until she serves him again."

"When I was a young man," said Sheyaka, "I have often called the fox for fun, when I had no intention of harming him. He is a keen and cunning hunter, but easy to fool when you know his weakness. I would imitate the squeaking of the larger field-mouse. He never hesitates, but runs directly to the place where the noise comes from.

"Once I saw him afar off, travelling over a burnt prairie. I lay down in unburnt tall grass, and gave the mouse-call. He came on as if he were very hungry, running at top speed, and I kept squeaking so as to make it seem as if there were many mice.

"When he reached the tall grass he sprang high as he came, and when he jumped clear over me I suddenly gave a war-whoop and waved my blanket. You should have seen how scared he was! He tried to turn back in mid-air and fell almost upon me so that I got hold of his tail. I laughed so hard that I could scarcely keep my hold, but the end of the matter was that he left part of his fine brush with me. I wore it for a long time as a hunting trophy."

The others laughed heartily, but Katola said: "Ugh, you were not fair with him, for you invited him to a feast and then gave him such a fright that he would always hate and fear his brother man."

"That is true; yet at times a hunter can with propriety play a joke upon a fellow-hunter," declared old Hohay.

"It is strange that none of the other animals like the Igmu, the great cat people," remarked Sheyaka, as if he desired to draw out Hohay, who had loosened the buffalo-robe around his loins and settled down with the evident satisfaction of one who has spoken his mind upon a disputed question.

"Toh, they are to the others as Utes to the other Red men," he replied at once. "They are unsociable, queer people. Their speech has no charm. They are very bashful and yet dangerous, for no animal can tell what they are up to. If one sees you first, he will not give you a chance to see so much as the tip of his tail.

He never makes any noise, for he has the right sort of moccasins.

"Igmu scatters her family in the summer. The old pair go together; the young go singly until paired. In the winter hunting they often travel within hailing distance, but not like us, the woman following the warrior. One goes up a gulch or creek while the other follows an adjacent creek, and they have a perfect understanding. They feed in common on the game they kill, and unite to oppose a stranger."

"Tell us something of the customs of the larger four-footed people, as the moose, elk, and bison," urged Sheyaka. "But it is time to smoke," he added, as he passed to the old man a lighted pipe.

"Ho, ho, kola; you know an old man's weak points, Sheyaka! I was about to ask for the pipe, but you have read my thoughts. Is it not time for a song? Can you not give us a buffalo or elk song? My stories will move with more life and spirit if you bring the animal people into my presence with your songs."

So Kangee sang a buffalo song, a rude yet expressive chant, of which the words went something like this:

"Ye the nation of the west—A-hay-hay-a-hay!
Ye the people of the plains—A-hay-hay-a-hay!
The land is yours to live and roam in;
You alone are preservers of life—
'Tis ordained from heaven that you should
    preserve our lives!"

"Oo-oo-oo-oo!" they all joined in the yelps which are the amen of savage song.

Hohay took one or two heavy pulls on the pipe, forcing a column of smoke through his nostrils, and handed it back to Sheyaka. He tightened the robe about him once more, and his wrinkled face beamed with excitement and delight in his subject.

"It is from these large and noble four-footed tribes that we derive many of our best customs," he said, "especially from the elk and buffalo people. But, boy, you have danced well! Your father dances like an old bear—where did you learn the art?"

These savage jokers were highly personal, but jokes were never resented in their life, so Sheyaka laughed heartily and good-naturedly with the rest.

"The buffalo and elk people are among the noblest on earth," continued Hohay, after the laugh was ended. "The grizzly is a drunken, mad fighter, who attacks without reason. He is conceited because he is well armed, and is continually displaying his weapons. The great cat is much more ready to mind his own business, but, after all, he is much of a coward. The wolf warriors are brave where there is meat. All these characteristics are shown also among men.

"The buffalo and the elk fight only for their people and their country. They do not hunt among other tribes, and where they live together in large numbers there are fewer quarrels than among the same number of men together. They never leave their children until they are able to take care of themselves.

"They have made everything possible to us in our free life. They supply us with food, shelter, and clothing, and we in turn refrain from needlessly destroying the herds. Their summer gatherings are the grandest sight I have ever seen.

"But I must stop, friends. There is one sad thing about all this. It has just come into my mind. The wild man is bad enough, but there comes another man—the paleface—who has no heart for what is dearest to us. He wants the whole world for himself! The buffalo disappear before him—the elk too—and the Red man is on the same trail. I will stop here, for it brings me sad thoughts."

He ended, and the others dropped their heads; not a word was uttered after this turn of the Red philosopher's logic. Hohay left the teepee, and the others followed him in silence.

GLOSSARY OF INDIAN WORDS AND PHRASES

an-pay´-tu lay wo´-yu-tay wa´-tin-kta mē-che´-chă u´-yay yō, *bring me food to-day.*

chăn-dee´ ō´-tă, *plenty of tobacco.*

Chă´-pa, *the beaver.*

Chă´-pă-wee, *the female beaver.*

Chăp-chin´-chă, *the young beaver.*

ē-nă´-kă-nee, *hurry.*

e-yă´-yă lō, *he ran away, he is gone.*

ē-yu´-hă nă-hon´ pō, *hear ye all.*

glē-chu´, *come down.*

hăn´-tă, *look out.*

Hă´-yă Tănk-ă, *Big Mountain.*

Hay´-kinsh-kah, *the spoonhorn or bighorn.*

hĕ´-chĕ-tu, *it is well.*

Hĕ-hă´-kă, *the elk.*

hĕ-hĕ-hĕ, *an exclamation of distress.*

hē´-nă-kă, *wait.*

Hē-tunk´-ă-lă, *the mouse.*

hē-yu´ yō, *come here.*

Hē-zee´, *Yellow Teeth—a nickname.*

hī, hī, *an exclamation of thanks.*

Hĭn-hăn´, *the owl.*

Hĭn´-pō-hă, *Curly Hair—nickname for yearling buffalo cow.*

Hĭn-tō´-lă, *Blue Hair.*

hō, *yes—denotes approval, or a salutation.*

Hō´-hay, *Assiniboine.*

Hoo´-tay, *Claws or Stubby Claws—nickname for a bear.*

Hoo´-yah, *the female eagle.*

ho-yă´, *run of fish.*

hō-yay, come on, *let us do it.*

hu´-kă-hay´, *come on.*

hŭn-hŭn-hay´, *an exclamation of surprise.*

Ig-mu´-tănk-ă, *the puma.*

Ig-tin´, Long Whiskers—*a nickname for a puma.*

ĭn ah´-jin, *stop or stand still.*

Kăm-dō´-kă, *Slaps the Water—nickname for a beaver.*

Kăn-gee´, *the raven.*

Kă-tō´-lă, *Knocks.*

kō-lă, or koda, *friend.*

koo´-wah yay yō, *come here.*

Mă-kē´-zē-tă, *Smoking Earth—name of a river.*

Măn´-ĭ-too, the wolf—*abbreviation of shunk-man´-i-too.*

Mă-tō´, *the bear.*

Mă-tō´-skă, *White Bear.*

mă-yă´-lă, *a steep place.*

mă-yă´-skă, *white cliff.*

Min-ne-tonk´-ă, *Great Water—name of a lake.*

Ō-pă´-gē-lă, *Fills the Pipe.*

Pă-dă´-nee, *Pawnee.*

Pēz-pēz´-ă, *the prairie-dog.*

Pēz-pēz´-ă tă ā´-yăn-pă´-hă-lă, *the prairie-dog's herald (the owl).*

Ptay-săn´-wee, *White Cow.*

Sē´-chăn-gu, *Burnt Thighs—nickname of a band of Sioux.*

Shă-ē´-yĕ-lă, *Cheyenne.*

Shē-yă´-kă, *the diver.*

Shun-gē´-lă, *the fox.*

Shun-gē´-lă pă-hah´, *Fox Ridge.*

Shunk-măn´-ĭ-too, *the wolf.*

Shunk-tō´-kĕ-chah, *the wolf.*

Sink-pay´, *the musk-rat.*

Sin-tāy, *Tail—a nickname.*

Sin-tay´-hă-dah, *Rattle Tail, the rattlesnake.*

Sin-tay´-ksă, *Bob-tail—a nickname.*

tă-chin´-chăn-ă, *fawn or lamb.*

Tă-dō´-tă, *Plenty of Meat.*

Tăk´-chă, *the deer.*

tă-kō´-jă, *grandchild.*

Tă-tănk´-a, *the bull.*

Tă-wă´-hink-pay-ō´-tă, *Many Arrows.*

tee´-pee, *lodge.*

Tē-ō´-lă, *Wounded in the Lodge.*

tē-yō´-tee-pee, *council-lodge.*

tōsh, *certainly, of course.*

tu-lă´, *an exclamation of satisfaction.*

tun-kă´-shē-lă, *grandfather.*

Un-spĕ´-shnee, *Don't Know How.*

U-păn´-ō-koo-tay, *Elk Point; the place where elk are shot.*

Wă-coo´-tay, *Shoots.*

Wă-dē´-tă-kă, *Brave.*

Wăk-pă´-ē-păk-shăn, *Bend of the River.*

Wăk-pă´-lă shē´-chă, *Bad River.*

Wăm-be-lee´, *the eagle.*

Wăsh-ă´-kă, *strong.*

Wăsh-tay´, *good.*

Wă-su´-lă, *Little Hail.*

Wă-zee´-yah, *the god of cold or winter; the north.*

Wē-chah´, *the raccoon.*

Wē-chah´-tă-wee´, *February—the coon's month.*

Wē´-tă-ō´-tă, *Lake of Many Islands.*

woo, woo, *a war-whoop.*

wō´-pă-tă, *place of killing or dressing game.*

Zē-chah´, *the squirrel.*

Zu´-yă, *warrior.*

PUBLISHER'S NOTE

This book was produced as part of the Publishing master's degree program at Western Colorado University, Graduate Program in Creative Writing. The students worked cooperatively to produce these fine new editions of worthy public-domain works. The intent is to bring literary classics to a new readership. For the enjoyment of a modern audience, some minor revisions to archaic terms or punctuation may have been made.

Because these works were written in a different time, some attitudes and phrasing may seem outdated to a modern audience. After careful consideration, rather than revising the author's work, we have chosen to preserve the original wording and intent.

ABOUT THE AUTHOR

Following the Santee Dakota (or Sioux) tradition of taking a new name after a major life event, Ohiyesa became known as Charles Alexander Eastman when he was fifteen and became more involved in European-American society. He graduated from Dartmouth College and Boston Medical School and treated survivors of the Wounded Knee Massacre in 1890.

In 1901, he published *Indian Boyhood*, a collection of

stories from his experiences growing up among the Santee in Minnesota, USA and Manitoba, Canada. He went on to publish twelve more books on Native American legends, autobiographical works, and political treatises. These included: *Red Hunters and the Animal People* (1904), *Wigwam Evenings: Sioux Folk Tales Retold* (1909), *The Soul of the Indian: An Interpretation* (1911), and *Indian Heroes and Great Chieftains* (1918).

He gave lectures on Native and European-American cultural cooperation and was involved in helping youth groups. He designed and helped set up youth camps and was a founding member of the Boy Scouts of America. He died in 1835.

ABOUT THE EDITOR

An editor, writer, and overall creative, Tammy Lewis received a BA in English from Brigham Young University and went on to write and edit articles, papers, and technical documents with aerospace scientists and engineers. She is currently pursuing a master's degree from Western Colorado University.

Whether in fiction or non-fiction, Tammy is always focused on the stories around her and in how to present those stories to the world so they can be learned from and enjoyed. Her latest projects include the republication of *Red Hunters and the Animal People* by Ohiyesa (Wordfire Press, July 2024) and *Feisty Felines and Other Fantastical Familiars* (Wordfire Press, July 2024).

WORDFIRE CLASSICS

The Lost World
The Poison Belt
by A. Conan Doyle

The Wolf Leader
by Alexandre Dumas

The Cthulhu Stories of Robert E. Howard
by Robert E. Howard

The Detective Stories of Edgar Allan Poe
by Edgar Allan Poe

The Jewel of Seven Stars (Annotated)
by Bram Stoker

From the Earth to the Moon and Around the Moon
by Jules Verne

The Complete War of the Worlds
The War in the Air
Kipps: The Story of a Simple Man
The Sleeper Awakes and Men Like Gods
by H.G. Wells

Mother of Frankenstein: Maria: or, The Wrongs of Woman &
Memoirs of the Author of A Vindication of the Rights of Woman
by Mary Wollstonecraft

We: The 100th Anniversary Edition
by Yevgeny Zamyatin

One Stormy Night : A Story Challenge That Created the Gothic
Horror Genre
by Lord Byron, Dr. John William Polidori, and Mary
Shelley

HOLIDAY CLASSICS

The Ghost of Christmas Always
by Charles Dickens & Kevin J. Anderson

The Santa Claus Stories
by L. Frank Baum

Our list of other WordFire Press authors and titles is always growing. To find out more and to shop our selection of titles, visit us at:
wordfirepress.com

facebook.com/WordfireIncWordfirePress
x.com/WordFirePress
instagram.com/WordFirePress
bookbub.com/profile/4109784512